# MARK OF THE
# BEAR CLAW

Janie Lynn Panagopoulos

*To Mindy —*
*In celebration of Michigan History!*
*J. L. Panagopoulos*
*05/05/05*

**River Road Publications, Inc.**

*Spring Lake, Michigan*

Hardcover ISBN: 0-938682-78-4
Paperback ISBN: 0-938682-83-0

Printed in the United States of America

Copyright ©2004 by Janie Lynn Panagopoulos
Illustration Copyright ©2004 by Jenifer Thomas

Library of Congress Control Number: 2004102806

*Dedicated to the memory of my friend and teacher*
*Nookimis Keewaydinoquay  (Woman of the Northwest Wind)*
*Margaret Peschel*
*1918-1999*

## Special Thanks

To my friend and teacher Nookimis Keewaydinoquay, "Grandmother Kee," for all that she has taught me, and to our mutual friend and sister WeTahn, Lee Boisvert.

To my good friend Lynn Kurtz for her help, and Michelle Willis, Program Director at the new Bay Mills Immersion School, and her husband, Mike Willis, Native Studies Director, Bay Mills Community College, Bay Mills, Michigan, for their help with proper translations of the Anishnabek/Algonquian language.

To my son Nicholas Panagopoulos for his help with French translation.

To the archivist and librarians at the Newberry Library, Chicago. To the archivists at the Clarke Historical Library, Central Michigan University, and the Bentley Historical Library, University of Michigan.

To the interpreters at Johnson Hall, New York; Old Fort Niagara, Youngstown, New York; Fort Stanwix, Rome, New York; and Fort Michilimackinac, Mackinaw City, Michigan; and Project Lakewell, Inc.

To Bob Mack, New Baltimore, Michigan, for providing such interesting information concerning Pontiac in Detroit.

# Contents

## OATH OF ALLEGIANCE TO GREAT BRITAIN
## AND HIS ROYAL MAJESTY: GEORGE II, 1760

*"I _____ swear that I shall be faithful and that I shall behave myself honestly towards His sacred Majesty George the Second, by the Grace of God, King of Great Britain, France and Ireland, Defender of the Faith, and that I will defend him and his in this Country with all my Power, against his or their enemies; and further I swear to make known and reveal to His Majesty, His General, or their assistants in place present, as much as depends of me all Traitors or all conspirators that could be formed against his Sacred person, his Country or his Government."*

## Chapter One

# MACKINAC
# JUNE 4, 1763

The isolated trail cut a sandy path from the shoreline through the forest. Pounding, moccasined feet broke the morning's silence as five young Native men sprinted across the cool, fern-strewn ground, not yet warmed by June's midmorning sun.

Makow followed after the runners. His heart, racing with fear, felt as though it would burst from his chest. From above, the familiar caw of the black crow—the storyteller—called down to him a warning, "Beware! Beware!"

Makow stopped. His eyes scanned the treetops for his protector, but could not find him. Makow reached up and tugged at the black spike of the crow's feather that hung knotted in his hair, making sure it was secure. Until that morning when he had been stirred from his sleep along the shore of **Waug-o-shance**, he had no knowledge of what was about to happen at **Fort Michilimackinac**. But now he followed five young **Odawa** warriors who had challenged him to join in a deadly game.

Along the sandy trail the shadows of the forest soon gave way to bright, sunlit rows of tiny green corn plants waving in the spring wind. Makow caught up with the warriors as they crossed the cornfield. They ran to take their place among their people to help finish what had been started by **Bwondiac** (Pontiac) a month earlier in Detroit.

Soon sun-bleached pickets of Fort Michilimackinac appeared, its English flag fluttering overhead. The last of the warriors turned to Makow and raised his fist in defiance against the English. He let out a sharp war-whoop bidding Makow goodbye and luck in finding the enemy he sought.

Makow slowed his pace and watched as the Odawas disappeared into a crowd of colorful and well-muscled warriors that had begun to gather outside the walls of the fort. They had painted their faces black and red, and covered their bodies with designs of totems and protectors. They were the Sauk from the **River Ouisconsin** beyond the **Lake of the Illinois** and the **Baye of the Punts**, Ojibwa from **Minissing Mackinac**, and now, Odawa.

The warriors were straight, lean, and strong like the baggataway (lacrosse) sticks they carried. The gaming sticks, Makow had been told, would be replaced by weapons once the warriors were inside the fort.

Makow watched and listened to the crowd while the warm morning sun cast purple shadows from the pickets down onto the field outside the fort where the game would be played. A scream of excitement in the form of a war-whoop pierced the air, breaking the secretive tension that grew from within the warriors' breasts.

The players, painted and feathered, divided themselves: the Sauk on one side near a post driven in the ground as a place of taking points, and the Ojibwa on the other, near their point post. Both tribes waited impatiently, restless for the deadly game to start.

From where he stood, Makow could see Indian women slowly making their way in through the fort gates one and two at a time. They smiled and laughed, talking cheerfully with the soldiers, careful not to give away the secret that would betray their husbands, brothers, and sons.

Indian women were welcome at the fort, where they sold their baskets, moccasins and maple sugar to those who lived within. On this warm, sunny morning, however, there was reason to be concerned about the women wrapped in heavy blankets.

As Makow watched, he was filled with a sense of pride in his people. Indians had the ability to see things that were ignored by others. The English could only see what they had time to see or what they wanted to see, while the Indian watched everything. No Indian woman would wrap herself in a blanket on such a warm, sunny morning. But the English did not notice.

The English also should have noticed the absence of the red knit hats of the Montreal traders. Today only the brave Charles de Langlade, who once led the Odawa against the English in Ohio, was seen with a few of his voyageurs walking around the open gates of the fort, smoking his pipe. Even from a distance, Makow could see de Langlade had a worried look upon his mixed French and Indian face. And soon he, too, disappeared with his men into the fort and the safety of his cabin.

If only the English could have learned to look with their eyes and not with their arrogance, Makow thought, they would not have put themselves in this danger or be so despised by his people. Grandfather was right. Before one could see, one must learn to look.

As Makow stood watching the gathering, he ran the toe of his moccasin over a half-buried rock. Stooping down, careful not to be seen, he dug into the sun-baked sand and pried it loose. It fit perfectly in his hand, a weapon that was meant for an English enemy. Makow concealed the rock under his crossed arms and made his way through the crowd, closer to the gates of the fort.

From inside, he heard the hollow roll of an English drum. Then suddenly, a blast from a cannon made him jump. "Huzzah! Huzzah!" shouted the soldiers as they tossed their three-cornered hats into the air. "Happy Birthday to King George!" cried one. "Long live the king!" cried another. "Huzzah! Huzzah!"

Makow observed Etherington, the English major of Fort Michilimackinac, as he marched out of the gate with his men to the lacrosse field to greet Minavavana, the Ojibwa chief. Etherington's bright red military coat with its many shiny buttons will make him easy to find when the battle begins, thought Makow.

As he edged his way through painted bodies and nearer the red-coated soldiers, Makow quivered with anticipation. Soldiers laughed loudly and began to gamble on the team they hoped would make them rich. Etherington soon joined them and exchanged coins. It was a day of celebration, the birthday of the English King George. The major had looked forward to this day of fun and relaxation for a long time, just as his enemy Bwondiac did.

Peering into the fort, Makow could see rows of small, square cabins lining the parade ground. The Indian women, he could see, were scattered throughout the fort, but they were not the object of his search. Soon he spotted pretty Angelique hurrying toward the safety of de Langlade's cabin. Makow hoped, with all his heart, for her safety.

Not far behind her, however, was the one Makow had hoped to find—his enemy. This English "dog" had nothing but hate in his heart for anything Indian. Makow smiled, satisfied to know his enemy had not escaped after all.

As he watched, Makow ran his fingers through his chopped, bushy hair and smoothed the crow feather knotted in the tangled mass. He wished he could have oiled his hair with bear grease and pulled it back tight with a leather thong, like a proper Odawa. His sunburned skin was naked and without paint. If only there had been time to prepare, he would have painted the design of the twin bear claws upon his shoulder. He was a warrior now and he must play the part.

As Makow watched, the proud painted warriors, he could hear the soft words of his mother whisper to him, "It is better to have peace, Makow. It is better to have peace." But those words meant little to him now;

it was too late. It was now Makow's turn to pay back the English boy who had given him so many insults.

For a moment Makow paused as a vision of the redheaded Scotsman named MacGinty flashed through his mind. Even though MacGinty had raised this English dog, his enemy, Makow hoped the kindly man had escaped and perhaps was even now at Waugo-shance with Makow's grandfather.

Tension grew thick as large groups of impatient warriors called out war-whoops and slapped their sticks together high in the air. They were anxiously waiting to honor the plan of the great war chief Bwondiac of Detroit.

A small leather ball was thrown into the air and the competition began.

The game itself was like a battle, with warriors leaping and falling over one another and men rolling to the ground and hitting each other with their gaming sticks. In an instant, one of the Ojibwa team, streaked with sweat and dust, scooped up the ball in his netted stick and threw it hard in the direction of the Sauk point post.

Major Etherington shouted and cheered with a loud voice, clapping his hands. On the playing field the warriors again scattered, running and shouting war-whoops. They slammed their bodies into each other and fell into a tangle on the ground.

As they scrambled to their feet, one of the warriors seized the leather ball in his net and hurled it high into the air and over the palisade into the fort itself. The surprised soldiers clapped in excitement and moved aside as warriors chased the ball through the gates of Fort Michilimackinac. Once inside, the warriors threw away their gaming sticks and grabbed the weapons concealed under the blankets of the women. The battle at Fort Michilimackinac had begun.

The soldiers' laughter soon turned to cries as ferocious war-whoops grew from inside the fort. The English were taken by surprise. In terror and confusion they began their struggle to save the fort and their lives.

Makow waited until the rush had slowed and stole silently inside, edging his way past the garden and traders' cabins toward the center of the fort. There, on the parade ground filled with fighting warriors and soldiers, he once again spied his enemy. He saw the trader's son running for his life when one of the Odawa warriors Makow had traveled with grabbed him by the waist and spun him off his feet. Kicking and screaming, the boy slipped from the Odawa's grasp.

Makow stood frozen amid the commotion and violence. With difficulty, he forced his terror back into his belly as he watched the wild scene before him. Soon, he saw the boy seized again, this time by his hair, and yanked backwards to the ground.

Finding his courage, Makow at last dashed through the smoke and cries, lifting his rock high overhead and shrieking out a war-whoop.

The Odawa warrior grabbed the English boy by his collar, pulling him to his feet and ripping away his shirt. The instant the shirt fell away from his enemy's body, Makow stopped in his tracks. There on the shoulder of that English dog was the mark of the twin bear claws.

The air seemed to be sucked from Makow's lungs as he stood frozen to the spot. This boy was no longer Makow's enemy; he was now the one Makow needed to save.

Makow grabbed the boy by his hair and yanked him from the Odawa's grasp. With his rock held high above his head, Makow made it clear he wanted this dog for himself. The warrior's eyes filled with rage, and he pounced forward at Makow with a blood-curdling scream. Then, just as swiftly, he turned and disappeared into the confusion of battle.

*Chapter Two*

# Detroit
# May 4, 1763

As Makow sat peacefully in his grandfather's wagenogan (lodge) near Fort Detroit watching the smoke curl up from the lodge fire, a fine black crow fluttered down the smoke hole to his side.

"Here," he said, placing his bowl of corn soup on the cattail mat before the bird. "You hungry? Try this, it is very good."

The large black crow cautiously hopped closer to Makow and the bowl and pecked greedily at its contents. Just then the lodge began to glow with the soft light from out-of-doors as Makow's mother pulled back the blanket flap and entered, carrying her sewing basket.

"Makow! What are you doing?" she scolded. "Do you not know how many times your grandfather and I have fasted so you might eat? And now you feed the wild birds? They always have more food than we. Mother Earth takes care of them without labor, unlike us."

Makow sat silent as his mother stomped her feet at the crow, who flapped into the air and out the smoke hole. In its place on the floor of the lodge lay a fine black feather. Makow quickly snatched up the gift and ran the spike between his fingers. Slowly he tied it behind his ear with a long strand of dark hair.

"Miig-wech, Andek (Thank you, crow)," he whispered as he smiled to himself.

"Mother, I think I will go down to the river to fish today. There are so many families here, perhaps I can find others to fish with."

"No. You will stay inside the lodge today. There are strangers here in the village. There is no telling what trouble you might get yourself into."

"But there is nothing for me to do. Even grandfather has gone out. Perhaps if I find grandfather, he will fish with me."

"It is not fishing you seek, Makow. I know you," responded his mother. "You have heard, as we all have, that the great war leader Bwondiac is calling a council of the Detroit Nations this day."

Excitement flashed in Makow's eyes. "I cannot wait to see him, Mother," he exclaimed. "It is said he brings a message from the prophet of the Delaware people, **Neolin**. A message of importance for us all."

"Makow, you have heard what I said. You will

have to wait,  as I want you to stay inside this day. There is a bad bird singing. Trouble is in the air, and I will not have you bring it to our lodge. If you keep the company of bad people, bad things will happen."

Angered by his mother's words, Makow jumped to his feet to confront her. "I can not believe you think Bwondiac is bad. He is Odawa and a friend to the French and to **On-on-ti-on**, the French governor.

"On-on-ti-on? The French?" questioned his mother.

"Yes, the French. Was not my own father from a long line of French traders from Montreal before the English dogs invaded and stole the lands of the Indian?"

"I will not have you speak that way in your grandfather's lodge," snapped his mother. "On-on-ti-on! On-on-ti-on! Never use that Iroquois name here again. Do you hear me?" she demanded as she stared into her son's dark eyes that were so much like his father's.

"What is wrong? There are Iroquois who are not our enemy now; some even live here at Detroit. Some even follow Bwondiac and do his bidding. You still hold on to the old ways. It is not like that now."

"You are young, Makow, and do not know all the story. You know only the parts that are good, those sung around the gathering fire. There will be a time when you will understand, a time that will make your heart cry when you hear the words, as it makes mine. To know and to remember this is important."

These words, however, were not good enough for Makow. He had many questions, questions that needed answers that never came. "Why is it then, Mother, that you have forgotten you are Odawa?" demanded Makow as he stood his ground.

"Do you not make elk skin coats and moccasins for the English Major Gladwin, at the Fort? Does he not call you Catherine, an English name of his liking? Were you not called O-gen-e-ba-goo-quay, Woman of the Wild Rose, by my father? Is that name not good enough for you now? Why have you forgotten?

"And why have you forgotten what the English have done now that they have come to Fort Detroit to live? Why is it you talk daily to those people, as if they hold something sacred that will help you discover your path?"

Makow's mother lowered her head, knowing how things must appear to her son now that he was old enough to have eyes to see.

"You are wise, my son, to see these things. But you do not understand. You are angry because you do not know what it is I seek. I forgive your anger." She turned from Makow, placing her sewing basket near the lodge fire. Makow stood watching, and hoping for answers to his questions.

"Makow," said his mother softly. "Twelve times the snow has fallen upon Noo-ki-mis Gii-zhik (Grandmother Cedar). Soon it will be time for you to leave this place with your grandfather, Lame Beaver, to journey to **Wa-gaw-naw-ke-zee** and beyond to Waug-o-shance to seek your path the way all your Odawa grandfathers have done. You should prepare yourself."

"I will not go!" snapped Makow. "This is my home now with the Odawa of Detroit and Bwondiac, not with my elders at that far away place."

"Makow, Wa-gaw-naw-ke-zee is the home of our people. It lies just beyond the place where the waters meet, beyond where the English now live in the fort built by the French. It is your grandfather's duty to pass on to you the knowledge of our ancestors. Lame Beaver is getting old. There are not many snows left before he will leave this earth. It is important that he helps you seek your path at Waug-o-shance, the place where he himself waited."

"No. You just want me to leave Detroit. You are afraid of Bwondiac and what he might do to lead our people against the English. Our people talk about you, saying that you make friends with our enemy. Why have you done this? What do you want from the English?"

"Makow, you need to be silent now," demanded his mother. "You do not know what you are saying."

Angrily, Makow turned towards the blanket flap. He would walk with his people, even though his mother had chosen to walk with the enemy.

As he lifted the blanket, Makow was surprised to find Lame Beaver, his grandfather, standing at the door in the bright sunlight. The old man gave Makow a wide gap-toothed grin, and motioned for the boy to move aside so he could enter. Looking down, Makow stepped back and the old man limped his way through the door. His long gray hair hung loose across his sloping shoulders and his movements were stiff and slow. As he pulled his red English blanket around him, he exposed a tattoo of twin bear claws on his sagging skin.

With a grunt, Lame Beaver lowered himself to the cattail mat and waited for his daughter to give him a bowl of warm corn soup from the kettle. He is getting older now, Makow thought as he watched his grandfather's slow movements. Although Lame Beaver's old ways sometimes did not make sense to him, Makow loved and respected his grandfather. This was the only father he knew, since his own French father had lost his life over the great falls that thunder (Niagara) before Makow's birth.

Lame Beaver slowly bent his stiff legs up under him, in preparation for his meal. Turning to Makow, he smiled and wiggled his knobby finger towards a **mocock** of maple sugar near the lodge wall.

Noticing this, Makow's mother snapped, "No, Makow. He eats too much sugar already. Look at his teeth. They fall from his head."

Lame Beaver smiled a jagged and broken-toothed smile at Makow.

"When his teeth are gone, how will he chew his dried meat in the winter? Will you chew it for him?" she asked Makow, knowing her son would do anything for the old man.

Lame Beaver smiled, ignoring his daughter's words and again motioned for Makow to get the lumps of sugar for his soup.

Makow looked at his mother and shrugged his shoulders, not knowing what to do.

"Makow," instructed his mother, who was now frustrated with both of them, "you should go down to the river and fish for our evening meal. Perhaps there you will find someone to fish with."

Surprised by his mother's words, Makow was glad to have permission to escape.

"And Makow," she added, "keep yourself from

trouble, as I have raised you with strength and purpose. Never forget this."

Makow glanced back at his mother as he slipped beneath the blanket to the out-of-doors.

*Chapter Three*

# THE VILLAGE

The camp at Fort Detroit was filled with many new Indian tribes. The Wyandot, from a village not far away, were the latest to join the gathering. Potawatomi from along the southern shore of the **O-wash-ten-ong** and from the river called St. Joseph had also gathered. There are more people than one could count, thought Makow, all here to listen to the words of the Delaware prophet Neolin, spoken by Bwondiac.

Makow knew that this place called Detroit was important to both the Indians and those who came here from across the great sea of tears (Atlantic Ocean). It gave travel access to the lakes that led to the great gathering of waters, the Mississippi. It was also an important post along the trade routes to lands where the four-legged creatures with the beautiful pelts lived. The Europeans so loved and desired these pelts that the lands and waters beyond had become a place of riches for many people. And Detroit sat at the doorway to these riches.

Fort Detroit itself, built by the French many lifetimes before, had filled with English after the end of the great war that had lasted seven snows (French and Indian War). In that war the French father of the Odawa lost to the English. He gave the English Indian lands that had been leased by the French.

The English had been at Fort Detroit now for two snows. This place, Makow had heard, completed a chain of English forts from Niagara to a place called Pittsburgh, making the redcoat soldiers strong enough to protect the lands and waters that lay to the north and west.

The tall pickets of Fort Detroit, over four times the height of a warrior, surrounded many English cabins, settlers, and soldiers. Outside the fort ran the bright blue Detroit River. And on either side of the river were the many cabins belonging to the French and Canadian settlers. Makow had heard that they all had taken an English oath so they could remain upon their lands to raise their gardens, orchards, and children.

All along the waterway, the villages of the Nations of Detroit also settled. Potawatomi lived a short distance downstream from the fort. Opposite them, on the other shore, sat the village of the Wyandot. The river here was not wide. It was a hard swim but an easy paddle, so the people traded and visited often.

Five miles upriver, along the eastern shore, the Odawa settled. They gathered from many places, like Makow's own family. Often during the summer, the great Odawa war chief Bwondiac left his home along the Beautiful River (Ohio River) and traveled north to camp near the mouth of Lake St. Clair, on the island called Isle aux Peches. Makow and his family, though they were Odawa, lived near the fort because of his mother's closeness to the English Major Gladwin. This closeness confused Makow and made him angry and suspicious.

As Makow walked through the village he noticed many fires were lit brightly for the middle of the day. Men sat together sharpening the blades of their knives while others, with great files, cut off the ends of their long hunting rifles. This was not a good sign. Perhaps his mother was right; perhaps there was to be a bad bird singing this day.

Turning his attention to the fort trail, Makow could see a crowd had gathered. In the center stood a tall, lean Native runner who had just arrived. He panted and glistened with sweat. Several women filled gourds of water, and the runner drank his fill. Then he reached into his pouch and pulled out a belt of **wampum** and a hatchet painted red. A sign of war, Makow thought, and he felt his heart beat faster.

The runner spread the word, interspersed with great war-whoops, that the war chief Bwondiac would soon arrive to speak to them about things of importance and that the people should prepare themselves.

From those gathered, Makow learned that four war belts of wampum had been sent in the four sacred directions by fast runners. Each delivered a message of the great council gathering. The runners were said to have gone to the river St. Lawrence in the north, to the Beautiful River in the south, the great water of tears in the east, and to the mighty Mississippi in the west. Each runner spread the word that the people should unite against the English and remember their French father, King Louis.

War belts, Makow's grandfather had once told him, were like burning sticks held over dried wood, sparking the fires of war wherever they were sent. This was surely true, thought Makow, as he watched the people who had gathered around the runner now rush to make preparations for Bwondiac and his war.

Children gathered wood, piling it high for the long evening fires and the dancing that would take place in celebration of Bwondiac's visit. Women filled great kettles of water from the river and placed them over the brightly burning fires that blossomed throughout the village in preparation for a feast. The Native villages around the fort at Detroit were now filled with activity and excitement. And Makow was glad to have escaped his mother's web of words to walk among his people. He would be careful to avoid his lodge until he had heard the great Bwondiac speak.

Makow's mother, it seemed to him, had always been fearful and acted as if she sought something beyond their everyday life. In his eyes, it seemed she lacked courage and strength. This was not a good thing for an Odawa, and Makow wondered if people thought the same of him.

Makow did know that at one time before his birth, his mother must have been brave. She traveled by birch bark canoe with his French father beyond the falls that thunder, and then to the Beautiful River and back. That, he knew, was many miles and would have taken much courage. But now, and for as long as he could remember, they had lived in this place, outside the Odawa settlement and close to the fort, so his mother could work for the English major. She washed Gladwin's shirts and sewed his elk and buckskins into moccasins and coats. She also spent many hours inside the fort talking with the English, always asking questions, making friends with the enemy of Makow's people.

Makow was angry with his mother for this. But when he asked her to explain, all she would say was, "I have lived in war. I have lived in peace. It is better to live in peace. Someday there will be a time you will understand. The English are people of knowledge and there are things I must learn from them."

What was it, wondered Makow, that his mother sought from the English?

As the sun began to drop in the sky, Makow could smell venison roasting over campfires in preparation for the feast. Then the distant sound of gunfire announced Bwondiac's arrival at Detroit. Losing himself in a crowd of people, Makow followed the path to the council fire to hear the words of the war chief and the message he brought from the Delaware prophet, Neolin, in the east. He knew it would be a gathering his mother would not attend.

Makow admired the warriors in the crowd. Some were wrapped in colorful blankets with hawk and eagle feathers swinging in their long hair. He reached for his own crow feather, knotted in his hair behind his ear. He, too, was a warrior.

Others gathered with shaved heads and only a tail of scalp-lock at the crown. "Less for an enemy to grab," the old men would say. Many had their faces tattooed with designs worked up with bear grease, soot, white lead, and vermilion. Some had feathers and stones thrust through their noses and others had circular designs, like the motion of a rattlesnake, spots and paw prints painted on their bodies. Tinkling hawk bells were sewn to their garters, and layers of beads, claws and bones on sinew decorated their chests.

Here and there a trader with his red hat, wrapped in his **capote**, and smoking a pipe, was seen mingling among the people. These traders of French descent had no more love for the English than the Indians did. Although they had taken an oath to stand at the side of the English and defend King George, they knew in their heart that someday their French father, King Louis, would return to claim his land and his people.

A roar of pleasure arose and hundreds of warriors now made a circle as the great chief appeared. Bwondiac entered from the east, in the direction of the sun trail, to honor the traditions of his people. He was followed into the circle by a row of his favored chiefs. They sat first, forming an inner edge of the council circle, and soon everyone sat.

To Makow, Bwondiac did not look tall, but he carried himself as a great warrior with a wide chest and powerful arms. His bearing was full of power and he seemed to grow before the eyes of the people. His bold

THE VILLAGE • 25

face was strong and his spirit was full of anger. His long hair, touched with the frost of fifty snows, lay straight at his shoulders and hung loose.

The voices around the circle grew quiet and Bwondiac silently walked in the direction of the sun around the inner circle, around the council fire. Slowly and with great strength in his voice, he began to speak.

Even though Makow sat near the outside of the great circle of people, he heard the war chief's strong voice clearly. In one hand Bwondiac held a wide belt of wampum, a belt, he said, the great father of the Indians, the French King Louis, had sent to him from the river St. Lawrence.

"This is a sign," he said, holding the wampum belt high above his head. "Our French father has heard our voices calling out against the bad English that steal our land, hunt our deer and beaver, and give us no gifts in return.

"The English think they own this land, but no man owns his mother. The English are not like our French father who gave us gifts of steel, powder, and cloth in exchange for the use of our lands for settlement, and our hunting grounds to trade for furs. The English are not like a misguided brother, that needs to be taught our needs. They are our enemy."

As they listened to the angry words of Bwondiac, no one dared to speak.

Next, Bwondiac spoke the words of the Delaware prophet Neolin, who had heard them in his fasting. "The great Maker of Heaven and earth made the trees, lakes, rivers and all things for his people. The land on which the Indian lives he made only for the Indian. Others should not live here without permission or without giving gifts to brighten the chain of friendship.

"It has been said that you have all forgotten your customs and traditions from your elders. You dress yourselves not in skins, but in cloth. You have traded for guns, knives, kettles, and blankets, until you can no longer remember a time without them.

"And worse yet, the English have brought upon us their two-horned devil—disease and the bitter water that drives you mad. The milk of the white man (liquor) imprisons you and will destroy you. This poison we take from them drowns the memory of all our ancient ways.

"We should now forget these things and live as our wise grandfathers once lived before the time of these strangers. The English rob you of your hunting grounds and drive away the game. They are not like the French, who have loved us and understood us."

Makow watched now as the great war chief again raised the wampum belt in one hand and in the other, the red war hatchet.

Suddenly, Bwondiac threw the hatchet to the ground and asked, "Who among the people are brave enough to pick up this hatchet for war? This war was started long ago when the first beaver pelt was taken from our land and sent across the great sea. This is the Beaver War. Who will pick up the hatchet to drive out the English and return us to the life our elders once lived?"

Bwondiac stood silent and looked angrily out over the crowd, then slowly walked in the direction of the sun around the council fire. When he completed his circle, he left towards the setting sun.

Makow could feel the emotions growing like a storm over the people. Other chiefs now stood and one at a time told the people their thoughts. All believed the nations must join fires so they would be strong like a well-woven mat and be able to save what they had left. Alone, they said, each tribe would be bent like a reed blowing in the wind.

Another chief said, "The English see the Indian as a tree that grows only for his use. We are angry the English treat us unfairly and leave Indians nothing to hunt or fight with except glass beads for bullets." These words stirred the hearts of many.

Thick clouds of anger began to gather around the fort and village. A white mist rose from the river, mingling with the dark smoke of the council fire. And from the sky, a black rain began to fall. With it came a smell that Makow had known only once, a smell that came from a deep crevasse in the ground that puffed the yellow stink of sulfur. His people had never known a rain like this before. It was a bad sign.

In fear the people covered themselves with their blankets and the council fire began to burn low. Many began to leave. It was then Makow noticed someone standing, staring at him from under a tree. It was Lame Beaver. Lifting his English blanket high over his gray head, protecting himself from the black rain, Lame Beaver motioned for Makow to join him. Makow dashed to the protection of his grandfather's blanket.

"It is not your place to be here," said Lame Beaver. "If your mother was to know, there would be a bad bird singing in our lodge."

"You will not tell her, will you, Grandfather?"

"Do you trust me?" asked Grandfather, looking intently at Makow.

"Yes, Grandfather, we are blood and you are my teacher. I trust you with my life."

"That is good, because in the morning you will need to give me that trust," the old man said as droplets of black, stinking rain pooled and dripped from the edges of his blanket onto Makow. "Come, now, it is time for us to go."

## Chapter Four

# ELK SKIN MOCCASINS

The next morning, Makow rolled over on his mat and pulled the blanket from his head. When he opened his eyes he could see his mother sitting near the lodge fire sewing a pair of moccasins for Major Gladwin. Sitting beside her was Lame Beaver, eating his corn soup.

Standing silently, Makow stretched and rubbed the sleep from his eyes and joined them by the fire. Makow's mother did not look up from her sewing. Makow could sense something was wrong. Did she know he went to the council fire? Looking to Lame Beaver, he watched as the old man's wrinkled mouth caved in upon the horn spoon with which he ate. Lame Beaver looked up at Makow, smiled and winked.

"Makow," said his mother softly, "I have something to tell you. There is something I must do. I have seen with my own eyes and have heard with my own ears the plans that are being made here at Fort Detroit. I, too, visited the council fire last night, before the black rain fell. I saw you both there. You know what was said."

Makow glanced at his grandfather, surprised by his mother's words.

"Makow, I know it is hard for you to understand that I have made friends with the English. I also know it will be hard for you to understand that I cannot let their lives be taken." Makow's eyes widened as he heard the words of his mother.

"You must understand, I do this only because there is something I must learn, and the English are the only ones that might help me."

"The English can help you with nothing," snapped Makow.

"You do not know what you are saying, my son."

Lame Beaver raised a shaky hand for Makow to be silent and let his mother speak.

"I have thought about this, Makow, and I have burned **kinnikinnick** in hopes of finding a better answer to what my heart is telling me. But there is no other way. I must warn Gladwin about the danger. I will see him this day when I bring him his new moccasins. I will only tell him not to let Bwondiac enter the fort with his warriors. I will not betray our people, only warn the English."

Lame Beaver hung his head and placed his soup bowl aside, sad in knowing there would be nothing that would change the strong heart of his daughter. She would have made a fine warrior, he thought, if she were a man.

"Lame Beaver, Father," she continued, reaching out and touching the old man's arm. "You must now take Makow to Wa-gaw-naw-ke-zee for his time of seeking. If you go now, you will both be safely away from Detroit and no one will blame you for what I do, if I am found out. If all goes well, I will try to find you at Wa-gaw-naw-ke-zee."

Lame Beaver could feel tears fill his eyes and roll onto his wrinkled cheeks as he nodded. He knew there was great danger in what she was about to do.

Makow watched as his mother turned to her sewing basket and took out a large, round stone. Then she handed it to him.

"This, Makow, is the first stone for your sweat lodge fire. I want you to take it. A gift from me." Makow touched his mother's trembling fingers with his and took the stone.

"It is heavy, like my heart, for what I must do this day," she looked into Makow's eyes sadly. "I found this as I walked in the woods. I heard the cry of the black crow, but when I looked he was no place to be found, only this rock at my feet.

"This is how I knew it was time for you to go.

This is how I knew it was right, in my heart, to warn Gladwin."

Makow could see his mother's lip quiver as she spoke. He knew she was taking a path that was difficult and required much courage.

"Daughter," said Lame Beaver softly, "you know there is more to tell your son and the story must come from you." He watched the tears begin to fall from her eyes. "It is time, Daughter, you must tell him now."

Makow's eyes narrowed. What did Lame Beaver mean? he wondered. All was silent in the lodge, except for the crackling of the fire. Makow watched his mother as she tried to find courage to match her words. From above came a fluttering sound of wings and a crow perched at the rim of the smoke hole, quietly looking down at them. The crow broke the silence with a great, loud caw, then flew away. Looking up at the empty hole, Makow's mother gently smiled and cleared her voice. It was time to tell her story.

"Makow, there was another time in my life, long ago, when two sons were born to me at the same time. One son was left for me to raise, the other taken in war by the Iroquois and English."

Makow sat silent, listening to her words—words she had never spoken before.

"Makow, this is why I say peace is better than war.

War separates families and breaks the hearts of women. This is why I made friends with the English. They have the answers that I seek. I know in my heart your brother still lives. I know the English will help us find him."

"Brother? I do not understand." Makow was stunned. "Why did no one tell me? And this is why you make friends with the English? Grandfather? How did I not know—"

"All this happened," explained Lame Beaver, "before you were old enough to remember. After you and your brother were born, your mother was ill and others cared for the two of you until she could regain her strength. I shall never forget that sad day," continued Lame Beaver.

"The woman who looked after you was a good mother. The woman who cared for your brother was not. She left him alone because of her fear, and it was then your brother was taken."

"The Iroquois," interrupted his mother, "became allied with the English. They came north in retaliation for a great battle that took place in the land of Ohio. It was then they invaded our summer camp. It was then your brother was taken. I know in my heart he is still alive, living among the English. He was a special child, and because of this I believe no harm could have come to him."

"Special?" questioned Makow. "How is he special?"

Makow's mother raised her hand to silence her son.

"Makow, it is this knowing in my heart that makes me warn the English. You must understand this. I know they will help us find your brother so he may be brought back to our family and the ways of his people. I also know that now it is time for you, too, to seek answers."

Makow swallowed hard and nodded. For the first time, he could see strength come into his mother's face. Perhaps her secret, held for so long, had filled her with fear and weakness.

From outside the lodge they heard the voices of many warriors gathering and beginning to sing a war chant. Makow felt the hair on the back of his neck rise up. Bwondiac's call to war had finally been answered.

Makow's mother jumped to her feet and helped Lame Beaver stand. Together they pulled back the blanket flap and saw warriors gathering near a great fire as singers circled them. A large pole was being driven into the ground in preparation for a war dance.

Makow also could see women pulling the bark coverings from their lodges while others gathered the small children, leading them towards the river to be taken to safety.

"There is no more time for talk," instructed Makow's mother. "I must go now and so must you. I have packed a bag of food for your journey. It should last until you get to Fort Michilimackinac; from there you can trade for more."

Placing Gladwin's finished moccasins inside her sewing basket, she looked for one last time at her son and father. "I must go," she said, trying to hold back her tears.

Outside, the chanting grew louder. Makow's mother wrapped her arms around her son, now almost a man. She knew in her heart that this might be the last time they would be together.

Makow hugged his mother in return. He did not want her to go. Now he knew it was not just for the lives of the English she made this sacrifice, but also for him and for a brother he had never known.

"Remember, my son," she said as she looked into Makow's eyes, "it is better to live in peace."

Lame Beaver reached out his knotty hands and touched his daughter's arm. "Yes, Daughter, you are right. It is better to live in peace."

Letting go of Makow, she wrapped her arms around the old man's neck, The two smiled with tears in their eyes and touched their foreheads together. "Instruct him well, Father. Teach him the truth. Teach him of his brother."

Lame Beaver lowered his eyes and nodded at the responsibility now put upon his shoulders. His daughter reached up and wiped away the tears from his wrinkled cheeks.

"Remember, you are my daughter, and I was once a great warrior," said Lame Beaver. "Be brave."

"I have never forgotten that, Father. Now teach my son."

Lame Beaver stepped aside as his daughter left the lodge carrying the basket that held Gladwin's moccasins. Makow and Lame Beaver stood silent as they watched her disappear into the growing crowd, the war chants growing louder around them.

*Chapter Five*

# ESCAPE

As soon as his daughter disappeared, Lame Beaver grabbed for his blanket and draped it over one shoulder. From the wall of the lodge, he lifted his large turtle pouch. "Come, Makow, we must hurry."

Makow handed Lame Beaver his long, finger-woven belt, and the old man wrapped it many times around his waist and over the blanket to hold it in place. Then he tied his kinnikinnick pouch and knife sheath to it. Makow rolled their sleep mats and blankets together, tying them with leather thongs.

Makow grabbed his leather travel pouch that held his flint and steel kit, knife, string and fishhooks. There, inside the pouch, he placed the rock his mother had given him, as he fought back his tears.

"Makow, we must hurry!" demanded his grandfather, as he motioned for Makow to retrieve the food bag his mother had prepared.

At the doorway, the two watched as the people gathered outside. Makow noticed the great war post had been painted bright red, the color of blood. Warriors formed a dance circle around the post and carried clubs, also stained like blood.

Just then the crowd parted to let an old man enter the circle. He carried a drum made from an old rum keg covered with stretched deerskin. As the crowd moved back, Lame Beaver motioned for Makow to follow him. Together they wove through the people, walking with the slow rhythm of the skin drum that called out like a great heart beating, pulling the people together. Makow could see the crowd of warriors begin to dance in swirling circles.

The cries of the dancers grew louder, and suddenly the first dead thud of a war club slamming hard against the post echoed throughout the camp. It was followed by another and another. Angry voices rang out, and the beating of the drum quickened. The emotions of the people rose fierce in every heart and the crowd became one.

Makow had never known such fear before. He heard his mother's voice inside his head. *Peace is better.* He was beginning to understand her wisdom.

Quickly, Lame Beaver and Makow passed through the camp to the water's edge, where hundreds of canoes had been drawn up onto the bank. Makow had never seen so many canoes before and did not know where to search for theirs. Here and there he saw women who seemed to have found their canoes and loaded children and household items into them.

"How will we find our canoe, Grandfather?" asked Makow. Lame Beaver, now moving quickly around the birch vessels, paused and removed his moccasins and the turtle pouch from his shoulder.

"Here!" he replied. "This is good." Lame Beaver stood at the bow of a sturdy-looking canoe near the water's edge. He quickly placed his belongings in it.

"Grandfather, this is not ours..." Lame Beaver turned abruptly to Makow for silence. Makow knew not to question his grandfather's actions. Removing his moccasins, he quickly dropped the food sack, travel pouch, and sleeping mats into the canoe. Together, they lifted it onto the water.

Lame Beaver, more agile than Makow had ever seen him, held on to the canoe as Makow crawled into the bow and knelt. Picking up a paddle, Makow dug its blade deeply into the mucky river bottom, holding the canoe in place for his grandfather. Lame Beaver climbed into the vessel and picked up a long paddle from the canoe's floor. Kneeling at the back, he pushed the craft out against the current, and together the two escaped along the waterway.

As soon as they no longer could see the great walls of Fort Detroit, they stopped and adjusted their supplies so the canoe would glide more easily through the water. Lame Beaver sat on the bedrolls, since his stiff knees made it difficult for him to kneel. Silently and swiftly the two paddlers worked together against the current, passing the island of the Hog. Makow had been told that long ago the Frenchmen put their hogs there to keep them safe from wolves. The hogs gave back a gift by clearing the island of the large number of snakes that lived there.

Next came the mouth of Lake St. Clair and Isle aux Peches, the summer home of Bwondiac. Makow was glad no one appeared to be on the island to see their escape. After paddling about two hours, Lame Beaver was exhausted and directed their canoe toward shore for a rest. A tangle of dark green forest looked like a good place to hide. As they drew near, Makow grabbed a low branch that jutted out over the water above his head to hold them steady.

Lame Beaver lay down his paddle and untied his kinnikinnick pouch from his belt. He removed a pinch of the sacred mixture and placed it in his hand. Makow carefully turned and watched as his grandfather softly sang an ancient song for safe travel, his voice carrying gently across the water. Then, in each of the four sacred directions, he let the kinnikinnick scatter on the wind and into the water.

"**A-ho!** Let it be!" cried Lame Beaver.

When he finished, Lame Beaver retied his pouch to his belt. He carefully reached down and scooped water from the lake and drank slowly. "Makow, it is good if you drink plenty of water. It will give you strength. Drink now."

Makow let go of the branch above his head, and the canoe gently bobbed upon the water. With his long paddle Lame Beaver steadied the canoe. Carefully leaning over the edge, Makow scooped handfuls of the cool, fresh water into his mouth and rubbed it over his face. It was good.

As he sat back upon his knees, the fingers of the tree branch above his head snagged Makow's long, curly hair. Startled, he grabbed at the branch that held him. Lame Beaver steadied the canoe as Makow tried to loosen his hair from the grasp of the branch. As soon as he freed some of his hair, other strands would catch and pull even harder.

Standing helplessly in the unstable canoe with his hair yanked straight up above his head, Makow did not know what to do. It was clear Grandfather could not move forward to help him without the canoe overturning. Frustrated, Makow pulled on the limb, in hopes it would break free. Instead, it snapped back and tore hair from his head. In pain, Makow suddenly lost his balance and tumbled out of the canoe into the water. The branch, still holding Makow, dunked him under the water then yanked him painfully back to the surface. In anger, Makow now pulled the branch harder. With a great cracking sound the limb splintered and broke, plunging into the water, with Makow still attached.

As Makow fought for a foothold on the mucky river bottom, Lame Beaver moved the canoe beside his grandson so he could grab on and steady himself. Slowly, the two made their way closer to the shore, where Lame Beaver climbed out and tied the canoe to the roots of the offending tree.

Grandfather led Makow to shore, dragging the tree branch, and sat him on a large knot of gray weathered roots. There the old man attempted to break away the fingers of the branch that had woven itself so tightly into Makow's thick, curly hair. After a short time, Lame Beaver looked at Makow, whose face wore much pain, and shook his head. He walked stiffly to the canoe and returned with his knife.

Carefully, one slice at a time, Lame Beaver cut away Makow's long hair, freeing him at last. The seriousness in Lame Beaver's face began to fade and a twinkle came to his eyes. A moment later he burst out in laughter. Makow's chopped hair now stuck out in every direction like a stack of corn stalks.

Makow ran his hand over his sore head and tried to flatten his hair, but it was no use. Hopping up from the root, he plunged into the water and watched as chunks of his hair and his crow feather floated away. "Eeee-ah!" cried Makow, and he dove beneath the green water in anger, swishing his head back and forth.

Lame Beaver laughed and loosened the tie of the canoe from the tree roots. Crawling in, he guided it away from shore, being careful himself to avoid the tree branches. When he reached Makow, he jabbed him with his paddle. Makow shook his head and pulled himself up into the canoe.

Lame Beaver silently paddled alone for a while as Makow tried to smooth his hair. But the curls popped up in all directions.

"You know, Makow," said Grandfather seriously. "This is something that has happened before, a long time ago. Perhaps this is a sign."

"A sign?" snapped Makow. "How could this have happened before? How could this be a sign?"

"Perhaps it is time you learn how you are like your father. Except today, Makow, you had good medicine with you."

Makow picked up his paddle and drove his anger

into the water. "I don't know how you could say this is good medicine, now that I look like a bush," he insisted.

"You will learn what I mean when I tell the story."

Lame Beaver paused. At that moment, they heard the distant cracking sound of flintlock rifles, carried on the wind. It was from Fort Detroit, now many miles behind them.

"The bad bird is singing, bringing us sad news," said Lame Beaver. "We must leave."

## Chapter Six

# BAPTISTE

Swiftly, Lame Beaver and Makow matched their strokes, putting distance between themselves and Detroit. Makow's hair no longer mattered as the danger of war pressed near. As Makow paddled, he could not help but wonder about his mother and worry for her safety. Yet he knew what she did took great courage—courage that only a few warriors could boast of. And now, would he ever see her again?

Lame Beaver's thoughts, too, were with the woman they left behind. Although he worried, he knew his daughter and knew her actions were not those of a foolish woman, but a brave one. These thoughts healed the stiffness that had been with him for many snows and gave him the strength to remember what it was like to be a warrior again.

The two paddled fast strokes for nearly an hour before Lame Beaver slowed his pace and called forward, "Makow, what do you know of your father?"

Makow paused for a rest and tried to flatten his hair as he thought.

"I know my father was a French trader from Montreal. That I know," responded Makow.

"Yes, that is true. He traded many good things to our people, and that is how I came to know him and how he met your mother. The French are not Indians, but they have courage. They are afraid of no hardships, and the dangers of the woods mean nothing to them. Only the fear of **smallpox** stops them. Your father was a man like this; a strong man in body and mind.

"He came many times to our camp along the O-wash-ten-ong, or **La Grande Rivera**, as he called it. He brought iron kettles, mirrors, needles and cloth for the women and lead, gunpowder, and traps for the hunters. He also had many bad French blankets that you could throw a rock through. The French always had bad blankets. English blankets are better. My blanket is English; it is the best." Lame Beaver smiled a jagged grin. Then he laid his paddle down briefly and drew his blanket up to help take away the chill of the water.

"One spring, when the ice had broken from the river, your father came to our camp to trade for furs and he met your mother. He gave her a mirror of her own and called her his "Wild Rose." That is why your mother's name is O-gen-e-ba-goo-quay, Woman of the

Wild Rose.

"Your mother liked him very much and when he left, your mother left in his canoe with him. They were married in the tradition of his country and would stay together forever.

"For two snows, I heard nothing of your mother and this man. Then one day she was brought back to her people, with you and your brother wrapped in a doeskin. A group of neutral Huron, themselves fleeing from the danger of battle along the Beautiful River, the Ohio, had found you all in your mother's canoe.

"It was a restless time when you and your brother were born." Lame Beaver paused for a moment. "It is still a restless time," he added.

Makow slowly turned to the old man who sat in the back of the canoe. This man had been like a father to him and had taught him all the things he knew about being a warrior.

Lame Beaver looked up at Makow. "Paddle!" he insisted. "This is not time for you to rest."

Makow dipped the blade of his paddle into the water, as Lame Beaver continued his story.

"The Huron, cousins to our people, knew your mother because she had visited their camps with your father to trade before you were born."

Makow felt a shiver run down his bare back and for the first time he felt afraid of his own story. He dipped his paddle into the water and listened carefully, wondering why no one had told him this story before.

"First, Makow, I will tell you about your father and how you are like him." Lame Beaver paused a moment and cleared his throat. He wanted Makow to learn from his words, though they would be hard for Makow to understand and even harder to accept. But it was Makow's story and he was at an age when he must listen and learn.

Makow dipped his paddle silently into the lake as he waited patiently for his grandfather's words.

Lame Beaver lowered his long paddle into the water, steering them along Lake St. Clair. "Makow, you know all stories must be told in their own time, like the stories around the winter fires told only in their season. I know you will have many questions that need to be answered," said Grandfather, "and I will answer them when it is the right time."

Makow looked out along the lake surrounding them. It was like a broad kettle filled to overflowing, and the forested shoreline was a jagged line separating the sky from the water. He had once heard it said that the water was so wide and the earth so large that a young wolf, circling the earth, would die of old age before he finished his journey. Makow now knew this could be true.

Grandfather interrupted his thoughts and continued. "Your father was called by his French name, Baptiste, but your mother called him En-ig-o Mi-hiin-gan (Singing-with-all-one's-might Wolf) or Loud Wolf."

Makow smiled at his father's name, but he knew this was what he was called. What about his brother? Was he younger? Older? What was his name?

"Makow, do you hear my words?" asked Grandfather. "Do you not think the name of your father is funny?" He knew what Makow was thinking.

Makow nodded his head. "Yes, it is a funny name, Grandfather.

"This is how you are also like your mother. She laughed at the name, too, and at your father. She said the first time she met your father along the O-wash-ten-ong it was because she thought there was a wolf howling loudly along the river in the middle of the day, and she wanted to see what magic made this happen. And there, instead of a wolf, was your father in his canoe, singing his paddling songs loudly and very badly. From that time on, your mother called him En-ig-o Mi-hiin-gan."

"Did it not make him angry to have such a name

given to him by a woman?" questioned Makow, for he knew this would have insulted a warrior.

"No, your father laughed with your mother. That is how she knew he was to be her husband. They both liked to laugh together. He was not like other men."

"No, he had a really bad voice," added Makow.

"Your mother told me in her tears, the day your brother was taken, what had happened to her Loud Wolf on the day he left this earth. Although I am an old man now, I remember it clearly. It was the first time I ever saw your mother cry tears of a woman.

"Your mother told me she and Loud Wolf, your father, were at Fort Niagara, which stands on a high cliff overlooking the lake named Ontario. This is where waters of the great lakes meet together.

"It was at this time a belt of wampum was shown to the people of Niagara, and they were told the story of the great battle of Pickawillany, in the land of Ohio."

"Was it like the belt Bwondiac held at the council fire?" asked Makow. "The council fire where the black rain fell?"

"Yes, the belt brought to Niagara, your mother said, was like that. But the strands of porcelain beads, your mother told me, were stained red with blood. That was a warning for all who could see to flee from Niagara to safety. The black rain that fell last night was also a warning. No one listens or sees them any more. When I was a young warrior, a sign like that would have brought fear to all the people. But today Bwondiac is stronger.

"Your mother said the day the belt was shown at the fort the sound of the great falls, many miles away, could be heard on the wind. Everyone knew that sound was heard only before a great storm was about to burst. And they knew that storm would be a war between our French father and the English king, over land that neither owned.

"The English were greedy for land and new trade routes and pushed beyond the Indian boundaries without permission. This was land the French had given many gifts to use, but the English simply took.

"We asked our French father to help us and he built a necklace of forts along the Beautiful River to protect our land. This made the English king named George very angry and there was a battle, one that drove the English away for a while.

"The battle, at Pickawillany, took place in the homeland of the Miami in Ohio, where they made friends with the English. A **metis** named de Langlade led our people against them. The only good that came from this was that the neutral Huron, fleeing from this battle, discovered your mother with you and your brother, adrift in her canoe on the Lake of the Eryes."

"What were we doing in a canoe?" asked Makow as he stopped paddling and turned to Lame Beaver. "What was my brother's name?"

Lame Beaver paused for a moment, ignoring Makow's question, and stretched his arms out. A cool breeze now blew at them from the north. They had canoed many hours and the sun cast colors onto the sky like the inside of a shell from the distant ocean.

## Chapter Seven

# NIAGARA

"We will need to find a place to rest for the night. Soon the current of the great river beyond will take all our strength. It is better to start fresh when the sun rises in the morning," instructed Lame Beaver.

Makow agreed, but he wanted to learn more about how he was like his father and about his twin brother, and why his family had been adrift in a canoe. It was as if this story belonged to someone else. "You tell the story, Grandfather, and I will watch for a place to camp."

"Make it a high place so we can watch over the water. Perhaps your mother will come."

Makow knew this was right, but the only high land he could see was a long way off.

Lame Beaver continued, "After your father heard that the French were going to battle the English, he felt the need to take your mother away from the French fort of Niagara, as she was great with child."

"But Grandfather, why were we adrift in a canoe? And what was the name of—"

"I must tell the story as it happened so you will understand. Someday, Makow, you will learn things only happen in the time they are supposed to happen. It is one of the great mysteries of this earth. So let me tell the story in its place."

Makow nodded. "You are right, Grandfather," said Makow as he paddled and listened.

"Your father, Loud Wolf, had a bad voice, but his heart was good. He took your mother in his canoe loaded with trade goods away from this danger. He was smart to listen to the warning.

"Your father made a plan to go to the fort at Detroit, where there were few traders at that time. One snow before, a famine and the disease smallpox chased the people away and took the lives of many. But time had passed and it became a good place for a trader with his family to get a new start.

"Your mother and Loud Wolf traveled up river to Niagara. It is a short river from its source at the Lake of the Eryes to the Lake Ontario. But this river runs swiftly over a rocky bed and falls in a white mist over the great rim of the falls that are deeper than the sky is high."

"I have heard of the great falls, Grandfather. It is there my father lost his life."

"It is true. On that day your mother said they could

hear the sound of a dull roar along the length of the river. It was a bad bird singing its song, and was a warning your father ignored that day.

"Together they paddled hard along the lower part of the river, against the current. With every swing of the paddle the current grew stronger, and so did the thunder of the falls. They traveled slowly. But at last they came to the long carrying place, the trail along the river bank that would lead them around the falls to Little Fort Niagara, and on into the Lake of the Eryes.

"Your mother said, at the carrying place, Loud Wolf brought their canoe along the shore and tied it tightly to a tree. The canoe pulled hard against the current of the falls above them. Helping your mother ashore to rest, he quickly unloaded the canoe and piled their goods along the portage trail. Hoisting the canoe upon his shoulders, he traversed the portage and returned to carry the goods and help your mother."

"Could they not make one trip with mother's help?" Makow asked. "Mother would never have allowed father to do all the work. It is not her way."

"Makow, your mother was round with child. It is a difficult time for a woman to travel and she was already carrying all she could. Now be silent or I will tell you no more!"

Makow nodded and continued to paddle.

"By the time they portaged to the top of the great falls, where their canoe and supplies waited, your father insisted that your mother rest while he put the canoe in the water and repacked. Your mother pleaded with Loud Wolf that it was not safe to pack the canoe so close to a place where the roar of the falls was still so loud. But Loud Wolf did not want her to have to walk any farther. He assured her it was safe, for he was close to the bank, where the waters were calmer.

"Loud Wolf tied the canoe to a tree branch that hung out over the water, and it bobbed up and down, pulled by the current. He knew that many voyageurs loaded and unloaded their canoes at this place above the falls. It had to be safe. After he loaded, he returned to help your mother down the embankment to the canoe.

"As they approached the canoe, your mother said she felt the chills of fear run up her spine, and at that instant she heard a loud snap that signaled the beginning of the long darkness that filled her life. The branch your father's canoe was tied to broke free and quickly pulled the canoe and trade goods into the current back towards the rim of the falls.

"Leaving your mother's side, your father rushed

into the water after it. He was able to catch hold of the canoe and pull himself in. Your mother called for him to come back and leave the canoe, but it was full of their trade goods to start a new life in Detroit, and your father would not let it go. He took his paddle, and being a strong man with arms like a bear, he paddled hard against the current."

"Makow, Bear Skin, is that where I get my name? My arms are strong like a bear? Like my fathers? Is that how I am like him? Is that what this story is about?" Makow interrupted in excitement, holding his arms high over his head with his paddle stretched out between them.

"No, that is not where you got your name or how you are like your father," snapped Grandfather, and then became silent.

Makow quickly lowered his paddle into the water as he realized he had interrupted Lame Beaver, again.

"Your mother said she could see your father fighting hard to turn the canoe to shore. But although he paddled hard and fast, the current and the branch the canoe was attached to pulled him downstream toward the falls.

"Your mother called to your father to leave the canoe and swim. But all they had worked for was in the canoe. The water soon began to flow faster as it neared rocky rapids. Your father crawled to the front of the canoe and tried to cut the leather thong that held him to the broken tree branch. But before this could be done, the branch snagged on a great gathering of broken trees hung up on rocks in the river, jerking the canoe, and throwing your father into the churning rapids.

"Loud Wolf reached out with all his might and grabbed hold of the tangle of branches. The water forced him under, and when he surfaced the branches snatched a tangle of his long, curly hair, yanking and tearing at his scalp, holding him tight."

Makow's grandfather paused for a moment as he remembered the sad story.

"Your mother said he twirled in the water, fighting to free himself. She crawled out along the shore, as far as she could, and tried to reach him. But it was no use. Your father reached out his hand to hers across the water just as the branches broke away and carried him downstream to the falls, where he was lost to the spirit of the thunder.

"Your mother said she made her way along the shore to the very edge of the falls where the river drops and slams onto the rocks far below. For a long time she watched as the wild water tumbled over the great rim. There was no sign of your father. The noise was so terrible, she said, even the rocks trembled, and it was a long time before the sound left her ears.

"Far below, the water tossed and foamed in a great whirlpool, throwing white mist high into the air and making a beautiful bow of color. Here birds flew in circles above the thunder, and it was hard for your mother to understand how anything of such beauty could cause such evil. But that is the way with nature, always in balance with two sides, and you must always know and respect them both."

Sadly Makow listened to Grandfather's words. He paused and ran his fingers though his badly chopped hair. Thinking about his own experience with a tree branch, he swallowed hard. Now he knew how he was like his father and why Grandfather was right when he said that good medicine had been with him that day. Slowly, Makow again began to paddle, thinking about all he had heard.

"It was a bad thing that happened to your father. I liked Loud Wolf. He made your mother smile.

"After your father was gone, your mother said she put soot on her face and hair and sang the death song in his honor for many days. Then some French traders your father knew from Fort Niagara passed by. They, too, were on their way to Detroit.

"The traders placed a wooden cross beside the

great falls where your father disappeared. Your mother showed them where the canoe that still held your father's trade goods remained lodged in the tangle of dead trees on the rocks. She offered them some of the goods if they would bring back the canoe and allow her to travel with them to Detroit.

"After much danger and hard work, the men were able to free the canoe and draw it to shore. Even with great sorrow in her heart, she was grateful for their help. Then one night, when they had reached the shore of Lake Erye, things began to change.

"Your mother was fast asleep on her sleep mat when the soft call of an owl opened her ears. She heard the men whispering around the campfire. She learned that the men were planning to take her canoe and trade goods and leave her stranded in the forest to find her own way to Detroit. After all, what could this woman, so great with child, do? Being an Indian, they said, she would be fine in the forest and be able to find her way alone. And with her trade goods they would be rich men in Detroit.

"When the men put their feet near the fire to sleep, your mother crept from the camp. Silently she loaded her canoe and escaped upon the lake alone. She paddled all night and all of the next day, hoping to escape these evil, greedy men.

"She said she put all her fear into paddling, stopping only for food and to make water. On the afternoon of the second day she noticed clouds gathering low in the sky and felt the cold wind of the north stir the air. She had little strength left, but she knew she was only a few more days' paddle from Detroit. For this reason she decided not to listen to the wind.

"As the sky grew darker, the waves began to wear white hair, and she knew it was time to seek shelter."

*Shelter!* thought Makow. He was so caught up in his mother's brave story, he had forgotten about watching for shelter for the night. Now Makow could see a high flat piece of land just up the waterway.

"Grandfather!" called Makow as he pointed the blade of his paddle to the shore with its high hill.

"Ah, this is a good place, Makow," he said and directed the canoe closer to shore.

"I will finish the story after we make camp," said Lame Beaver with a tired smile. His lame legs and stiff bones had had enough of the canoe for this day.

*Chapter Eight*

# SHELTER

Once along shore, the boy and the old man unloaded the canoe and carefully pulled it onto a grassy slope. Pulling on their moccasins, they tracked into the shadows of the surrounding woods and found brush enough to cover and hide the canoe from anyone who might pass.

Makow took the food sack, his travel pouch, and the rolled mats and blankets up to the top of a high grassy hill that overlooked the lake. From there they had a view of the waterway, which stretched as far as they could see.

The sky had turned a tired gray-blue, yet there was no sign of rain as Giwedanang, the star of the north, was already clearly shining in the sky. Makow scattered pine boughs and placed their mats over them. Next he unrolled and spread out the sleeping blankets.

"This will make for a good sleep," said Makow proudly. "And we can watch out over the water—perhaps for mother." And perhaps for danger, he thought silently.

"It is a good camp, Makow," said Grandfather as he grunted and lowered his stiff body to the mat and pulled the food bag to him. The evening dampness made the devils dance in his joints. "Sleep will be a welcome visitor to my bones this night," he thought aloud.

Makow had one last thing to do before the purple shadows closed around them. Opening his travel pouch, he removed his flint and steel to make a fire. Searching the ground, he found chips of wood, strips of wig-wass (birch bark), and dried tree branches. He was careful not to include hemlock or pinewood that would crackle and throw sparks.

In the shadows Makow found the greatest prize, an old rotten tree with its wood turning to dust. He gathered a pile of wood dust and birch strips, then knelt and began striking the stone flint against the steel. Tiny sparks popped and snapped brightly into the air. He continued to chip away the flint until a spark finally ignited the rotten wood dust. With his face close to the little blue whirl of smoke, Makow blew softly and steadily until a tiny flame ate a strip of birch bark. It was now large enough for him to begin feeding chips of dried wood. Soon, Makow had a fire to warm his grandfather.

"You are more like your father than you know," said Lame Beaver as he yawned and stretched in the warmth of the fire. "If you were all Indian, you would have made fire from wood. But you use flint and steel as if you were born with it in your hands. Your French blood sings first in your veins, Makow."

Makow stopped and looked at his grandfather, now stretched out before the fire. "But Grandfather, you make fire with flint and steel. I have never seen you make fire any other way."

"One day, I will teach you to make a proper fire with only wood like my grandfather taught me and his grandfather taught him. It is an ancient way."

Makow looked at his fire and wondered what was wrong with using flint and steel. Wasn't this fire hot enough to cook a meal and warm tired bones?

"I remember the first time I looked upon you as a baby. Your hair, which was long and covered your head, was light and bending like your father's. I said to your mother, 'This one is French. Throw him back!'" Lame Beaver chuckled a little as he remembered.

Makow was surprised by his grandfather's words, but knew he was only joking.

"Did my brother's hair bend?" asked Makow.

"No. He was darker and his hair was flat and he was quiet—more like an Odawa. I was surprised your mother didn't call you Little Loud Wolf. When you cried, you were very loud."

Makow grinned. "No, she named me Mako-waian, bear skin. It's a name I don't understand, unless I was a strong little bear cub."

Grandfather chuckled, "No, that is not why you are named that, Makow." Lame Beaver smiled his broken-toothed smile and placed the food sack between them. He rummaged through the sack, which was filled with dried meat mixed with nuts, berries and fat, hunks of dried and salted fish, and even a great loaf of white bread given to Makow's mother from the kitchen of Major Gladwin at Fort Detroit.

Finally Lame Beaver seemed to find what he had been searching for. He pulled out a small, tied bag. He opened it carefully and grinned. Inside were a few chunks of hard maple sugar, his favorite. "Ah!" he smiled and showed the prize to Makow. "For me!"

They both ate dried venison from the bag, but it took Lame Beaver a long time to chew. Suddenly, the old man grabbed at his jaw in pain. Makow watched as his grandfather spat blood, meat, and an old brown tooth into the grass.

"Oh!" he moaned, holding his mouth and sitting very still. After a few moments he put his dried venison back into the sack and pulled off a nice piece of crusty white bread. Slowly he picked at its soft insides.

"I will miss that old tooth," said Grandfather sadly to let Makow know he was all right. Then he shrugged his shoulders. "It is hard to get old and lose your teeth. Maybe your mother is right. Maybe I do eat too much of the sugar she makes from the sap of the maple tree."

Lame Beaver took the open bag of maple sugar at his feet and wrapped it tightly, placing it back into the food sack. Then he reached into his turtle shell bag and pulled out a small doeskin pouch. He grinned as he loosened the strings and looked up at Makow. "Someday, if you are very lucky, you will have lived long enough to own a pouch like this," he said, shaking it at his grandson.

Thinking perhaps his grandfather had a small rattle inside, Makow stretched over and peeked into the bag that Lame Beaver held open. It was full of Grandfather's old broken teeth!

Makow pulled back and squinted his eyes in disgust. Lame Beaver laughed loudly, and then reached over to find the tooth he had spat out. Wiping and polishing it on his blanket, he dropped it into his bag. "See, I have not lost my teeth. I have them all in the pouch. You see, when I die, I want all my parts to be

buried together, so I may walk my path complete."
Lame Beaver chuckled and closed the bag, shaking it
to make the teeth dance.

"Grandfather, I hope I never have a bag like that,"
insisted Makow as he stretched out his full belly, now
round enough to play like a drum.

Lame Beaver leaned back on his elbows and
stretched his legs out in front of him. "It is good,
Makow," he said with a smile, "to live so old that you
must collect your teeth in a doeskin bag."

"Grandfather, tell me the rest of the story as you
said you would. You stopped when my mother was
trying to make it to shore before the storm, before
my brother and I were born."

"I will tell you only a little more, Makow, as I am
ready to close my eyes to this day.

"Your mother said as she paddled on the great lake,
the wind soon came upon her and clouds blew by
faster than she could paddle. The white hair grew
long on the water and she said she could hear the
voices of the Thunderers in the sky. Trying to steady
her canoe, she pulled kinnikinnick from her turtle
pouch and scattered it on the wind. No sooner had
she finished, she said, than a great finger of white
flashed across the sky. It was then she first felt the
pain of her children wanting to join her in this world."

Makow smiled, happy to have Grandfather tell him this story.

"Your mother tried to paddle toward the shore, until her pain was so hard she could paddle no more. She did not cry out. As you know, a mother that brings her children silently into this world, without showing pain, gives them her bravery and courage."

Makow nodded in agreement.

"Unable to go any farther, she made a nest in the bales of trade goods and lay back in her canoe with the wind blowing around her and waves splashing in. There your mother bore her pain bravely in silence upon the water, and brought you and your brother into this world."

"We were born in the water?"

"I do not see webbed feet on you, Makow. You were born in your parents' canoe, someplace on the Lake of the Eryes."

Makow smiled at his grandfather's joke.

"She used the water in the bottom of the canoe to wash you and your brother, then wrapped you both in the great warm arms of your father's capote to keep you safe.

"Soon, the long-haired waves pushed her canoe to shore before the rain. Those waves were kind, and brought her to a place not far from the camp of our

Huron cousins. She said it was your loud voice that called the Hurons, and for that she was very grateful you were like your father."

Makow sat staring into the fire, listening. His grandfather jabbed him with a knobby finger and smiled. "The Hurons carried you both, along with your mother, back to their camp, since your mother was very weak. By the time the rain came upon them, she was burning with fever.

"Our Huron cousins cared for the three of you for many suns. When your mother was finally well enough to travel, she offered them trade goods in payment for bringing you all to Detroit.

"After she was safely at the Odawa camp in Detroit, she discovered I, too, had moved my camp there."

"She must have been glad to see you, Grandfather," commented Makow.

"Yes, she was, but it did not take away her sadness for your father. And it took a long time before she had her strength back again."

"Did my mother know she would have two children?" asked Makow.

"What a silly question! What person would know the answer to that question, any more than a woman would know if she was to have a boy child or a girl child? No one has that magic in them to know such things."

Makow shrugged his shoulders. It was a silly question, he thought to himself.

"Did mother tell you which of us was born first?"

"Yes, she said the Odawa was born first because, like a warrior, he wanted to challenge the storm."

Makow hung his head. He had never thought of himself being last or looking like his French father. He was Odawa and had always thought of himself looking like everyone else. To now think of himself as someone different was upsetting. He reached up and tried to make his bushy hair lie flat.

Finally Makow stood up. He stretched his long legs and yawned, looking up where the stars brightly pierced designs into the night sky. He wondered if his mother was safe. Perhaps she left after she warned Gladwin and followed them in another canoe. Perhaps Gladwin, in exchange for his safety, told her where to find his brother. Makow looked out over the dark water but found no one there.

As Makow looked up, something in the sky caught his attention. A deep red and yellow glow lit the southern horizon. It was coming from Detroit.

"Look, Grandfather," urged Makow as he pointed.

Lame Beaver groaned, pulled himself to his feet, and searched the darkness. Reaching out, he put his arm around Makow's shoulder.

"Tomorrow, we must put much water between ourselves and this place. Now that the first strike has been made, attacks will fall like hammers across the land, from the great sea to the Mississippi. We must put our hurt into the paddles and be strong, Makow. Come now, let us find sleep."

As they lay on their blankets, Lame Beaver rolled over several times, unable to get comfortable. Pulling back his blanket and sleep mat, he rubbed his hand through the pine boughs and over the grass. With his knotted fingers, he dug in the ground and found the rock that kept him from his sleep.

Prying it loose, Lame Beaver felt it carefully. It was of medium size, round, and had no cracks. Another rock for Makow's sweat lodge, he thought, and laid it beside his mat. Smoothing his bed, he settled himself and quickly and fell asleep, snoring softly to the call of the owl and the splashing of the lake.

*Chapter Nine*

# THE JOURNEY

The next morning, Makow awoke from his sleep to hear the wind dancing in the trees around him and the beating of heavy waves as they splashed hard against the shore below the hill. Sitting up, he discovered his grandfather picking berries and small nuts from the **pemmican** inside the food bag.

Makow lay still and watched the old man's wrinkled face move up and down as he chewed. It must be hard to eat, Makow thought, with so few teeth.

Grandfather glanced over and caught Makow watching him. "I am glad you could join me this morning, Grandson. The sun will be high in the sky soon if you do not move faster. Today we begin to paddle up the river that leads into Big Fish Lake, the Lake of the Hurons. It is a long paddle against the river's current. It is better to start early before the sun is too high."

Makow sat up and rubbed the sleep from his eyes. The sun was barely above the lake, but he knew there were many sleeps of travel before they would reach Wa-gaw-naw-ke-zee.

"Here, I have something for you," said Grandfather.

Makow reached out to Lame Beaver, who dropped the rock into his hand.

"Another rock for the sweat lodge fire?" asked Makow.

The old man grinned. "It was meant for you. It kept calling me from my sleep last night, until I released it from Mother Earth."

Makow rolled the smooth stone in his hand. It wasn't as heavy as the one his mother had given him, but it would work. He reached into the food bag, grabbed a piece of dried venison, and stuffed it into his mouth. His mother had packed enough food to keep them until they nearly reached Wa-gaw-naw-ke-zee. But although her dried meats and pemmican were always good, Makow thought it would have been nice this cool morning to have some warm corn soup.

"Miig-wech, Grandfather," said Makow. "Grandfather, why is it so important to gather certain rocks for the sweat lodge fire? Why not find them when we arrive? It would be easier, since we wouldn't have to carry them."

Grandfather chewed and swallowed a piece of the

English bread with some berries. When he finished, he reached over to Makow's head and put his hand on his hair, trying to make the cut ends lie down flat.

"Hmm," said Lame Beaver. "Hair is not good. We will try to fix it later. Maybe we will cut it all off, maybe use bear grease."

"Did we bring bear grease?" questioned Makow.

"Always have bear grease. Pemmican is full of bear grease. We can use that. Now finish your meal. I will tell you the story of the rocks once we are on the water."

Makow hated the thought of using the bear grease from the pemmican. It did not smell so good, and they would have to pick the nuts and berries from it first. Still, using his grandfather's sharp hunting knife to shave his head didn't seem like a good idea to him either.

Makow rubbed his hands over his hair, feeling the jagged ends sticking up in all directions. I wish I had flat hair like my brother's, he thought.

After they ate and packed their belongings, Makow and Lame Beaver pulled the canoe from the brush where they had hid it for the night. From there they carried it to the water. Before he crawled into the canoe, Makow dunked his head in the cold water to smooth his wild hair. The wind was cold against his bare, wet skin.

Makow thrust his paddle deep in the mud to steady the canoe so his grandfather could climb in. Then, pushing off against the shore, the old man directed them out into the lake and toward the mouth of the river.

The current seemed to grow stronger with every swing of the paddle, and the old man and boy knew it was important for them to paddle quickly, so they would not be carried into submerged rocks. Together they struggled, trying to match each other's movements.

Grandfather soon called to Makow, instructing him to keep the pace while he pulled his blanket around him. Without Lame Beaver's paddle helping to move and direct the canoe, Makow's muscles strained. How difficult a journey it would be without his grandfather's help, Makow thought, even though he is an old man.

Lame Beaver adjusted his belt around his waist, pulling his blanket in place, and again joined Makow. Together they pulled against the current, slowly moving their vessel forward. Silently, each dug deep into the water for two hours until they found a place to rest.

As they approached the riverbank, Makow

watched carefully for rocks that might lie just beneath the water's surface, waiting to bite a hole into their canoe that would take hours to repair. Seeing none, he glanced overhead to make sure there were no hanging branches to pull him from the canoe and steal the rest of his hair.

Once on land, the pair secured the canoe lines tightly to the roots of an old tree. The current continued to pull at the canoe, and everywhere Makow looked there was movement. He knew they had not made good distance that morning, and wondered how many suns it would take them to reach the Lake of the Hurons.

Paddling upstream was hard, and Lame Beaver stretched his fingers, popping the joints in his aching hands. Makow also stretched and twisted his sore muscles, trying not to think of the many miles that lay ahead.

Kneeling along the river's edge, Lame Beaver scooped up the cold water. "Drink," he instructed Makow. "Water will give you strength. It is an important thing for a young warrior to remember."

Makow had never been called a young warrior by his grandfather before. Now that he had, he liked the idea.

Stooping beside Grandfather he took long cool

drinks that he quickly decided did make him feel better.

After the two had rested, they climbed back into the canoe and continued their upstream paddle. As they made their way north, the river seemed to slow and Makow could tell they were making better time. Finally, the third day on the river, Grandfather pointed into the distance and announced that the great Lake of the Hurons was within sight.

Once in the lake, Makow marveled at the beauty of the shimmering water. But a strong wind made paddling difficult, and after a short distance, the pair began to look for a place to rest. Grandfather directed the canoe toward shore, and Makow again scouted the shallows for dangerous rocks.

# *Chapter Ten*

# REST

On shore, Makow wanted to run and stretch his legs, but the dense woods around him made it impossible. He decided his one option was to walk along the shore.

As he set out, Makow looked back to check on his grandfather, who he expected to be finding a comfortable spot for a nap. Instead he saw the old man pull the food bag out of the canoe. Makow smiled. Now that he has no teeth to eat with, Makow thought, he is always hungry.

Makow walked along the lip of the land scattered with thick brush and ferns that waved and scratched at his bare legs. He watched as gulls, resting from the wind, bobbed up and down on the waves. It seemed to Makow to be like sitting in a cradle rocked by a bear. But the birds did not seem to mind.

Soon, Makow came upon a bush that was loaded with ripe, red berries. He watched as tiny bees hovered over them and sampled their sugar. Bees must be very powerful, Makow decided, since they are not swept away by the strong gusts of wind from the lake.

Perhaps that was why he had heard honey would make a warrior strong.

When the tiny bees moved away to another bush, Makow quickly picked as many berries as he could, stuffing them into his mouth over and over again. They were a welcome change from the dried venison.

When he had filled his stomach, Makow cupped one of his red, sticky hands against his bare skin and filled it to overflowing with berries. Then carefully he made his way along the shore and past the bobbing gulls to his grandfather.

Makow found Lame Beaver sitting along the lake's edge, his feet dangling in the water. "Grandfather, look what I have brought you," called Makow, certain the old man would be pleased to have such soft, sweet berries to eat. Makow squatted slowly, careful not to drop any of them. But when Lame Beaver looked up, Makow could see red berry stains all around Grandfather's wrinkly mouth.

"Oh, sweet berries," said Grandfather, smacking his stained lips and putting his hands out for another treat. "Miig-wech, Grandson."

Makow looked surprised. Not only had his grandfather found his own bush, but he had not brought any berries back for him. He watched Lame Beaver eat his berries, smacking his lips in pleasure. "These are very good sweet berries, Makow. Miig-wech."

"Ma-how (You're welcome), Grandfather." Perhaps he is beginning to see me as a man, Makow thought. It is time I take care of myself, and him as well. Besides, I can chew venison, and that is difficult for him.

"Grandfather, will you tell me now why the rocks we collect are so important?" Makow sat down and dangled his feet in the water beside Lame Beaver and continued, "I know they are important for the fire. And I know, after I spend three days of fasting and thinking in the woods alone..."

"Thinking?" Lame Beaver interrupted. "You speak like you are not Indian. When you go to the woods to fast, you don't hold on to your own thoughts. You must seek. That is when thoughts and images find you. The woods are much like the schools where the English and French children go. You, too, must go to school and be an eager student."

"Yes, Grandfather," said Makow. "And after I am in the woods for three days, I go to the sweat lodge to cleanse myself. Is that right?"

"Yes, it is a way of cleaning you from the inside to the outside. All Indian peoples, from all nations that I have heard of, use the sweat lodge."

"All Indian people? This I did not know."

"Makow, there are many things you do not know.

It will take many snows to find out, as it has me. And Makow, even now, with frost in my hair, I still learn. And when I am gone, you must remember these things taught to me by my elders, so that you can teach the young ones who will follow after you. Now continue."

"After I sweat in the lodge, next I plunge myself into the great Lake of the Illinois and become clean to walk my path in life as a brave. Is that right?"

"Yes, this is all right. Now, do you know my purpose?" asked Grandfather smiling, showing his pink gums and broken, brown teeth.

"To teach me how to find my path, and to find my answers? To guide me and help me?"

"I must teach you the things you need to know. I must help you understand your purpose and your importance in life.

"You must learn when you enter the sweat lodge, you should do so only with a clear, clean mind. You cannot hide troubles in your heart. You must be ready to let go of the bad things, such as anger, jealousy and fear. Then your heart can be filled only with good things and doing what is right for others."

"Do you think I will find my brother someday? Do you think he is still with the English as my mother has said?" asked Makow.

"When it is time, your brother will reveal himself

to you and you will know him. An English soldier told your mother, not long ago, that a Scottish trader who looks like a bear has a child he raises. But that child is not his and they say the child looks Indian. He is said to have been taken near Detroit many sleeps ago. The child now travels the trade routes from Montreal to Mackinac. This story has given your mother hope."

Makow's eyes grew wide. "Why did she not tell me of this? Why did we not go to Mackinac to find him?"

"In everything there is a lesson and a time. It would be difficult to find this man, as he travels many miles along the waterway. And perhaps this child that was taken is not your brother. But if it is, we will find him, and we will know him.

"You must learn many lessons. It is then things will become clear, and once you have learned these things, there is no man who can take this knowledge away."

"You said we will know him. How will we know him? How is he special that I will know him?" asked Makow.

As they spoke, a crow flew out of the woods, perched above their heads, and called down toward them.

"A-ho," said Grandfather. "Look, it is time to leave.

The crow comes out of the woods because the wind grows quiet. He is telling us to move on. He is a wise winged one, the crow, and knows many things."

Makow stood and dusted the dirt and grass from the back of his legs. But the dirt clung to his hands still sticky with berry juice. The crow called down to Makow, as if laughing.

"I like Andek. I think he likes me, too. Perhaps he is the symbol I will paint on my drum when I grow older."

"Perhaps. But it is no surprise the crow is around you now. He is the story teller, and often appears when one gathers stones." Just then the crow cawed again and sprung from the branch into the gentle breeze of the lake, and flew away.

"Look, Makow," Grandfather pointed above their heads at a black feather that floated gently down onto the surface of the lake.

Makow quickly waded out into the cool water, reaching again and again for the feather that drifted on the waves, just beyond the tips of his fingers. Finally, leaping forward in the water, Makow captured his prize.

"I think the crow knew I needed a new feather," a dripping Makow called to his grandfather, holding the quill for him to see.

"I think the crow knew you needed to wash berry stains from your skin and smooth your hair," said Grandfather, chuckling and rocking from side to side to loosen the tightness that grew in his knees.

"Me? I needed to wash the berry stains from my skin?" Makow joked, wading back toward Grandfather and splashing water at him.

"Makow, stop!" warned Grandfather, as he moved away from the splashes. Makow bent into the water, holding tightly onto his feather while he splashed water high into the air.

"Makow, you get me all wet."

"I am just trying to wash the berry stains from your mouth, Grandfather." The two laughed and Grandfather stiffly bent over and splashed his wrinkly face and rubbed his skin until it was clean.

"Is that better, Grandson?"

Makow smiled. It was better.

"We need to go now. The water is still, and the wind is going to sleep in the warm sun," instructed Lame Beaver.

Makow slipped the crow feather into his chopped hair and loosened the leather ties that held the canoe. Carefully he walked the canoe through the water, toward his grandfather. It gently rocked on the waves as Makow held it tightly. Grandfather stepped in and paused, balancing his weight. Makow teasingly jiggled the canoe, just enough to make Grandfather catch himself. He scowled at Makow for his trick. After Lame Beaver positioned himself in the rear of the canoe, he picked up his paddle and moved the canoe a little farther from shore for Makow to enter. As Makow started to lift himself on the **gunwales**, the old man took his long paddle and swiftly swung the canoe out, pulling it from under Makow. Losing his balance, Makow splashed backwards into the lake.

Lame Beaver laughed and laughed as Makow surfaced and blew a long stream of water at him. Makow jumped to grab the canoe, but not quickly enough. His grandfather drove his paddle hard into the water and pulled the canoe farther away. Missing the canoe again, Makow went splashing under the surface.

"Grandfather, stop!" Makow shouted, trying to run and catch the canoe as the water pulled hard against his legs. Lame Beaver continued to laugh, but finally stopped paddling. He held the canoe steady for Makow, who, soaking wet, seemed to bring half the lake into the canoe with him.

Swinging his wild hair like a dog, Makow cried, "It is too bad, Grandfather, I get your English blanket so wet." Grandfather quickly dropped his paddle and folded his blanket tightly behind him, placing it near the sleep mats.

Recovering from the fun, Makow picked up his paddle and began to match Lame Beaver's movements, stroke for stroke. Now the wind was sleeping, and it was easier to paddle against the lake. Gradually the pair picked up speed until they were moving as quickly as the beat of a war drum. Their bodies worked hard, but it made them both feel strong. The motion reminded Lame Beaver of his younger days and made Makow feel like a warrior.

*Chapter Eleven*

# LESSONS

Makow smiled, glad the trip would take many sleeps. Deep within, Makow began to understand that his grandfather and mother were right. There were many things he had yet to learn.

Makow paused for a moment, thinking of his mother. It would be better if they were all together. But for now he would follow his mother's wishes and his grandfather's directions.

"Makow," called Grandfather. "Look in the water." He pointed his paddle alongside the canoe. Floating in the water was a crow's feather. Instantly Makow reached behind his ear to discover his was no longer there. Could this feather have followed them the long distance from their resting place?

Grandfather reached out his paddle and guided the feather near the birch bark, where it bobbed up and down and waited for Makow. Leaning out of the canoe, Makow carefully plucked it from the green water, running his fingers up its spine to smooth and shape it.

Placing the feather behind his ear, he realized his own hair needed to be smoothed and shaped as well. He pushed his hand against his hair, trying to flatten it as much as possible.

"Miig-wech, Grandfather."

The old man smiled and continued to paddle.

That evening, they again made camp along the lake on a high piece of ground. Makow was laying out the sleep mats when he realized his grandfather had disappeared into the shadows. When he returned, the old man's arms were full of wood and many gifts of nature.

"I will teach you now to ish-ko-de-quay. How to make a proper fire," he said, as he stooped over and laid his treasures down. With a grunt, he lowered himself to the ground.

Taking a long, wide piece of soft, dry cedar wood, he held it up and turned it to make sure it was strong. "This is the base. Makow, do you have your knife, fish line and hooks with you?"

Makow nodded and got up to search his traveling pouch. Under the rocks his mother and grandfather had given him, he found a ball of thin leather string. It was a fine fishing line his mother had cut for him last winter from a deerskin she had tanned. In the ball he had stuck a half-dozen barbed fishhooks. From a beaded sheath with the design of twin bear claws his mother had made, Makow took his small, sharp knife and handed both the knife and fishing ball to Grandfather.

Makow watched closely as Grandfather took the point of one of the fishhooks and dug a circle about a half-inch deep into the soft, dry wood. Next he took Makow's knife and gently ran his finger over the sharp blade. "Sharp! That is good. You take good care of your knife. It is a dull knife that is most dangerous."

Makow smiled. He had heard his grandfather tell him that over and over since he was very young.

With the knife, Lame Beaver cut a narrow groove from the hole to the edge of the cedar board. "This board, we will keep. It can be used over and over. That is why the old way is good. Nothing is wasted."

Next, Lame Beaver took a stick of dry hardwood, about a foot long and as big around as his finger. He removed all the bark with the knife, making a soft point at both ends, so either end would fit into the hole in the cedar board. From another small square piece of hard wood, he used his knife to dig a little hole that would fit onto the stick he had just shaped.

"These things we keep to use again, too." Grandfather looked up at Makow to make sure he was watching carefully.

Picking up a long, skinny, springy branch cut from a sapling, Grandfather measured out a piece of the leather fishing string, longer than a man's foot, and cut it with the knife. Bending the branch into the shape of a bow, he tied each end of the branch with the ends of the string so that the branch would stay bent.

Lame Beaver held the bow up and examined it to make sure it was strong. "Fire-bow," he said simply as he showed it to Makow.

Makow nodded as his grandfather began piling fine dry pine needles and curls of birch bark on the dry cedar board. He sprinkled the pile with the dust of a rotted tree limb. Then, taking the stick with the soft pointed ends, he laid it against the leather bowstring and wrapped it tightly with the slack leather. Carefully, he placed the stick into the hole on the cedar board that was surrounded by tree dust, birch curls, and pine needles.

With the stick in place, Lame Beaver put the hardwood block on top of it and held it with his left hand. He adjusted the bow and string and then began pulling the bow back and forth with his right hand. As he did, the stick began to turn with lightning speed. Soon, a tiny wisp of gray smoke, created by the friction of the bow, rose from the burning wood dust in the hole of the cedar board.

"Makow," the old man directed, "give the smoke more wood dust and pine needles." Placing the material into the groove that was cut to the edge of the board, Makow fed the tiny fire. His grandfather sawed with the bow until a spark finally took the dust and needles.

Quickly Lame Beaver pulled the stick from the hole and scooped the small fire into a pile of birch bark strips and wood chips. He blew gently on the pile until the flames grew tall and began to eat small branches and hunks of wood. When the fire was finally strong, he looked up at Makow and smiled. "This is the way the elders made their fires."

Makow smiled, noticing that the firelight danced upon his grandfather's face and made a mask of his wrinkles. It seems to reflect the wisdom he has gained in all his long life, Makow thought.

"And look, Makow. We can use everything over and over." Grandfather took the cedar board, stick, bow, and block and placed them all neatly in a pile near his turtle bag. We will take this with us when we leave. Sometimes making a fire is hard when there is only one," the old man continued. "But you will learn. I have done it many times alone."

Makow was quiet as he thought about his

grandfather's lesson. It took many steps to make a fire as the elders did. If Bwondiac and the Delaware prophet had their way, all would have to make fires like the elders.

Then Makow thought about the new way of making fire. It was much easier to use flint and steel, and one person could easily do it. Makow looked at Grandfather's neatly arranged bundle of bow, stick, and block, and knew it wouldn't fit into his turtle pouch, no matter how he tried. But Makow's flint and steel fit very easily inside its own brass box. He could also carry old material or wood dust so it was always available and dry. And the pieces were so small they fit easily into his travel pouch.

It was nice to learn the old ways, Makow thought. But maybe his French blood did run first in his veins, because the flint and steel made more sense to him. He hoped Bwondiac would not take away the flint and steel.

"So what do you think, Makow?" asked Lame Beaver. "It is easy, and everything is from wood. Oh yes, and from a bit of your mother's tanned leather. When I was young and my father first taught me how to make fire, he made me go dig spruce root to use instead of leather. I bet you are glad I didn't make you do that."

Makow smiled at Grandfather and agreed. But had Grandfather forgotten he also used a fishhook and a steel blade provided by traders? Perhaps, Makow thought, Grandfather is a little French, too.

Hungry from a day of paddling, the two soon turned their attention to the food sack. Lame Beaver pulled out a piece of dried fish with a hunk of white bread that was now getting hard. Makow ate several pieces of dried venison and a handful of pemmican. Everything tasted good.

Happy because he had taught Makow to make a proper fire, Lame Beaver suddenly remembered something else. Reaching for the pile of wood he had brought from the shadows, he pulled out another rock for Makow.

"Here, I found this in the roots of Noo-ki-mis Gii-zhik. This is special as she gave us her wood for our fire and a rock for your sweat lodge. I left an offering of kinnikinnick to thank her." Lame Beaver gave Makow a broad, jagged grin.

## Chapter Twelve

# STORIES

"Now," said Grandfather, "let me tell you the story of the rocks."

Makow reached forward and took the rock from Grandfather's rough, callused hands and looked it over. It was heavy and black, with no cracks or marks. It was a good rock.

"Miig-wech, Grandfather. This makes three rocks for the sweat lodge fire."

Grandfather smiled, "Ma-how, Grandson."

To Makow it seemed his grandfather was enjoying this journey as much as he was. Perhaps, he decided, the old man was remembering his own time of seeking, many snows ago. Now if only his mother were here, it would be even better. Makow hoped she would soon find her way to them. He also hoped that she had changed her mind and did not warn Major Gladwin. Makow wondered if his grandfather felt the same, but he did not ask.

"The rocks," continued Lame Beaver. "Some collect them from many places over a period of time, as we are collecting them. They are to be treated carefully. No throwing, no dropping. You see, the rocks are called 'the elders.' They were here even before the Indian. Rocks have many stories to tell, as they are old and wise. They have traveled from deep inside Mother Earth to join us. Rocks will be here even when we are here no more. Someday they may even tell our story to the people yet to be born."

Makow liked that. Someday, someone might know his story and the story of his mother and grandfather, perhaps even his brother.

"I have been told in the old days, stories were not known to the two-legged ones, we humans. Can you imagine life without stories? But, stories did not come to the two-legged ones until a great rock met Andek, the black crow."

"Ah, so that is how the crow came to be known as a storyteller? From a great rock?" asked Makow.

"Yes, that is right. A lonely crow with a voice that did nothing but chatter all day stood on a great rock and would not leave. The rock got so tired of hearing the crow chatter and say nothing, it finally decided to speak to the crow to see if it would be quiet for a moment and listen. To the rock's surprise, the crow did become quiet and listened. So the rock told the crow a story.

"After that the crow often returned and heard many more stories told by the great rock. Crow began to repeat the stories, over and over. One day, a boy on his fasting quest listened carefully to the crow and the boy understood.

"When the boy returned from his fast and cleansed himself in the sweat lodge, he thought about the stories and they became even clearer. When the boy plunged himself into the cold lake, the stories grew bold in his head. Later on, he shared the stories with the people and told everyone about the crow and the great rock. And that is how the crow became known as a storyteller, by perching upon a great old rock and listening quietly.

"You know, Makow, the crow likes to talk as much as you. He is very loud, too. Perhaps you will paint his image on the head of your drum when you are older."

Makow smiled and ran his fingers behind his ear and found the black feather secure in the bends of his hair.

"Remember, when you hear a crow's loud voice, it is a sign a story is calling for you, and stories teach you many things. Sometimes it is a lesson, sometimes it is a warning."

"Perhaps it will teach me about my brother," said

Makow.

"If you listen with your heart, it might."

"I wish it would tell me if my mother is safe," said Makow as he looked up at Grandfather.

"Makow, your mother is doing what she feels in her heart is right. It is hard to say what is right and wrong for another. You just have to know what is right for you. And if your heart and her heart are right, you will always be together. Always do good, from the heart."

Makow thought for a long time about Grandfather's words. He would also listen more closely to the crow's caw to hear if it had a story about his mother.

"So now, do you understand about the rocks? They were the first storytellers and taught the crow, and the crow teaches the people."

Makow nodded. Stories were a good gift, he thought.

"That is what I have been told, Grandson. Treat rocks with respect for they have been around for a very long time. They still tell their stories to the crow, and sometimes to humans from the sweat lodge fire, if they listen.

"I also know when a rock is heated for a sweat lodge, it glows like the rising of the sun, like the time rocks were first pushed from inside Mother Earth. That is an old story, too.

"These are just things I have been told, as I am not a storyteller," said Lame Beaver. He sat back and ran his finger over the broken outline of his teeth and pink gums.

"Grandfather, stories fall from your lips like stones into a pond. You are a very good storyteller, but I think when you were young, you were a better runner. Mother told me that story."

Lame Beaver looked at Makow and smiled.

"Mother said before snow came to your hair and you walked with a limp, you ran for the people during times of danger to bring news and sometimes even to save lives."

"That was a long time ago," said Lame Beaver with sadness in his voice. "I ran for the people because I was chosen. My legs were long and straight and my body strong. Makow, that is one way you are Indian. You are like me, with long, straight legs. The legs of the French are often short. Someday you may need to run swiftly on those long legs."

Makow wondered if someday he could run to save lives.

"Forty times the leaves have fallen from the birch tree since I last ran for the people," continued Grandfather. He proudly sat up straight and put the food sack aside. "You see, it was a long time ago and our people, the Odawa, had gone to battle far in the land of the Illinois. I was called to be a shadow in the woods, to hide myself during the time of battle so I could watch the fighting.

"This was a difficult thing for me to do, not to take my place in battle beside my brothers. But I was asked to run. It was my duty to report back to our people all that took place.

"The battle was long and hard. Our people did not do well, and many were lost. When all was finished, I crept away, but was followed by an enemy.

"I ran swiftly through the woods toward home, carrying word of our defeat. But behind me ran the enemy. He followed me through the swamps, along the lakes, and across rivers. He was like an angry wolf as he chased me, never letting me go. He also was smart, because I could never see him in the forest or on the water. I only knew he was there, and he made me run harder, faster, and longer to reach home.

"I was only a day's travel from our camp when I stopped to rest for the night. But my enemy was a stronger man than I. He did not rest. He ran ahead, until he saw the smoke of our people's lodge. There, in the trail bent in the meadow grass that led to our camp, he dug a deep hole and covered it with brush, so none would know what he had done. It was only then he lay down to sleep.

"The next morning, I left my resting place before the sun was awake and made my way toward camp, running swiftly across the meadow. Suddenly I sensed my enemy behind me, his moccasins cutting the grass before him as his feet barely touched the ground.

"Soon he was so close I could hear the sweat fall to the ground. It made me run faster. I did not know he was chasing me into his trap until he stopped and gave a loud war-whoop in victory.

"It was then my foot broke through the cover of the trap, dropping me downward into a pit. I could not get up, and rolled over in great pain. The white bone of my leg stuck through my skin, and my foot turned itself in a direction it was not made to turn.

"Crying out in pain, I could not stop my voice as it escaped. I was surprised and angry at my weakness. And because I cried out, my enemy gave another loud war-whoop, celebrating my weakness.

"I thought my heart would explode with fear, and my whole body ached as I lay in the pit waiting for my enemy to take his trophy. He peered down at me, giving another war-whoop of victory. His face was painted red with black circles around each eye. His long hair was pulled high on his head in a knot

"He pulled his great, long hunting knife from his belt and prepared to jump in upon me. Then I heard, from behind him, the heavy thud of a tree branch strike him. The blow knocked him off his feet, and as he tried to stand, he dropped his knife, which stuck deep in the ground in the space between my fingers.

"It was then I heard the shrill cries of the women from our camp. The warrior was not so brave when a shower of rocks flew through the air at him. I hoped the arms of our women were good, so none would fall in on me.

"The sound of many moccasins running swiftly upon the grass passed by. Then all was quiet. I waited for a long time and worried I had been forgotten, but the women returned. They all laughed and told the story of their victory, how they could see only the bottom of the warrior's moccasins as he ran away into the forest, afraid of the Odawa women.

"Working together, the women lifted me from the the trap that had been set for me. I was in much pain, but the women had showed so much courage, I could show no less, and I did not cry out.

"They made a **travois** for me and pulled me back to camp. They set my leg and placed medicine of honey and plants on my wounds. It was many sleeps before

I could tell them the story of our brave men in battle. They cried the death song for their men, but were happy they had saved me from the enemy.

"I was happy, too. But when my leg healed, it was known by all that I would never run for the people again. With my limp, the only thing I could do was to become a good trapper for our people. That is why they changed my name from Running Wolf to Lame Beaver."

"How did the women know you were out there so they could save you?" asked Makow.

"You see, there was a pretty girl named Red Hawk Woman. She had good eyes. She was given the job of sitting in a tree at the edge of the meadow to watch for the return of our warriors. For two days she watched, and on the morning of the third, she could see a handsome swift runner being chased by another.

"She climbed from her tree and warned the women, who prepared themselves for battle. She was very brave. She had beautiful eyes that sparkled in the sun and good, strong, white teeth," said Grandfather, who paused and rubbed his tongue over his own broken teeth.

"That is why," he continued, "Red Hawk Woman became your grandmother, and that is why I have my nice knife today. This is the knife of my enemy," said Grandfather, pulling his knife from its sheath for Makow to admire. "It is the one my enemy dropped into the hole beside my hand, nearly cutting a design in my fingers." Carefully he ran his thumb over its sharp edge.

"It is a good knife, and your grandmother was a good wife. I should have thanked my enemy," laughed Grandfather. Then he saddened as he remembered how the English smallpox had taken the life of his brave Red Hawk Woman many snows ago. "She was a good wife," he repeated softly.

Makow was silent thinking about the story he had just heard. It was one he had never heard before. There was so much he needed to learn from his grandfather.

"Grandfather?" Makow asked timidly. "Will you tell me another story? Will you tell me the story of my name?"

Lame Beaver shook his head. "That story must come in its time, Makow. We have many more days of journey ahead of us."

## Chapter Thirteen

# Rocks!

Over the next few days, Makow and his grandfather awoke before the sun grew red out of the Lake of the Hurons, and made their rest stops as short as possible. By now the threat of Detroit was far behind, and they found no lodges or canoes along the waterway. In their effort to paddle the 250 miles of the Lake of the Hurons, Makow's arms grew strong, and his grandfather found his youth as he worked the stiffness from his joints.

The shores were low along the broad waters of the Hurons, making it hard to find a good place to camp. But each night the pair selected the highest ground possible. Makow always watched the water until sleep found him, hoping in his heart to hear the sound of his mother's paddle.

In most places the shoreline was covered with heavy forest. As they paddled, Makow's grandfather often pointed out deer and black bear that came to the water's edge to drink. At one point they passed through a large and beautiful bay at the mouth of the **Sau-ge-nong** River. Grandfather explained that the Odawa had made their camp there before they had moved to Detroit, and before that, a tribe called the Ossaw-gees had lived there.

On another night, the pair made their rest at what Grandfather called Odawa Bay (Tawas), north of the Sau-ge-nong. It was a safe harbor with few rocks, but the black flies and mosquitoes were evil. Makow made a low, wet fire full of smoke that night to keep them away. Grandfather squeezed the bear grease out of what was left of the pemmican and rubbed it on their skin to keep the bugs from biting. Makow was glad to leave that place.

Days later, Lame Beaver pointed across the lake in the direction of the rising sun and told Makow that if he had the eyes of a hawk he could see the bay of many islands (Georgian Bay). Makow squinted hard and said he thought he could see it.

"This is how you are like your grandmother, Red Hawk, with good eyes, if you can see the bay from here," said Grandfather with a laugh.

It was then Makow learned that the bay of many islands was three suns' paddle across the Lake of the Hurons. Grandfather had tricked him.

That night the pair camped along another beautiful bay with its stony shore and crashing waves

(Thunder Bay). They unloaded their canoe some distance away from the rocky coast and, piece by piece, carried their belongings ashore. Then they carefully carried the canoe ashore, turned it on its side, and braced it against canoe paddles stuck in a small patch of sand to make a shelter.

Clearing stones away as best he could, Makow laid a deep layer of cedar boughs on the sand and covered them with their mats. There he and Lame Beaver slept until a slice of red sun grew from the lake and opened their eyes in the morning.

Along this stretch of the Huron shore, Makow found another rock for his sweat lodge fire. Since his travel pouch could no longer hold all his rocks, he carefully placed them in the center of the canoe to keep them safe. Every day, he loaded and unloaded them, always thinking it would be better to collect the rocks at Waug-o-shance. Grandfather only laughed as he watched Makow, for he knew the moving of the rocks made this young warrior stronger.

At last, they approached the northern end of the Lake of the Hurons, and, as the shoreline curved to the west, many islands began to appear. Grandfather named them all, explaining that he had once hunted or fished on them as a young warrior.

The winds now came from many directions and

the water rolled and churned. As they struggled with the wind and squinted in the late afternoon sun, Lame Beaver decided they should camp near the mouth of the river called Cheboygan, nearly opposite the island of Bois Blanc.

As they headed toward shore to make camp, the choppy water slapped against the canoe and bounced them around. Makow tried to watch for submerged rocks as he fought the wind. But the bright sun and churning waters made the task nearly impossible. It was not until he drove his paddle hard against a rock that he knew it was there.

Frantically Makow tried to push the fragile birch bark canoe away from the rock, but in the process jammed it into another one on the other side. Immediately water began to leak through the tear in the canoe.

Lame Beaver plunged from the canoe into chest-deep waves, steadying the vessel as much as he could. He instructed Makow to jump out to lighten the load. Makow did as he was told and shivered in the cold water as they struggled to pull the broken vessel to shore. With the canoe's belly sagging deeper and deeper, the pair knew they must work quickly before the waves completely overtook it.

The moment they were close enough to shore,

Makow grabbed the soaking bedrolls, the English blanket, the food sack and their travel pouches and dragged them to safety while Grandfather held onto the canoe as best he could. Everything, including the rocks that filled the bottom of the canoe, had to be carried to shore.

By the time Makow finished, only the lip of the canoe was still above water. With all their strength, he and Lame Beaver turned the canoe on its side as the powerful waves slapped against the boat and nearly knocked them off their feet.

Little by little, the pair emptied the water from the canoe until they could lift it, upside down, onto their shoulders. The bottom of the broken canoe shone in the setting sun as they finally reached the safety of the shore. Once on shore, they propped it on its side to dry and braced it so that it would not fall over in the wind and be damaged further.

Although the two were exhausted, both knew they had no time to rest. Makow quickly started a fire with his flint and steel while Lame Beaver began spreading out their belongings to dry. Makow watched as his grandfather frantically searched through his belongings until he found the doeskin bag that contained his old teeth. Looking up at Makow, he rattled the bag in the air and smiled. "Don't want to lose any of me," he said with a chuckle.

The problem now was food and comfort. The little food that was left would soon spoil now that it was wet. The shore, a mixture of sand, tall grasses and rocks, would make for a poor sleeping night, and their blankets would take many hours to dry. As darkness came, the two stayed near the fire and used the damaged canoe to break the wind from the lake. As they looked out into the darkness, they soon noticed stars begin to fall from the sky, as if poured from a moccasin.

"Look, Makow, the rabbit must be at work again," said Grandfather as he pointed upward.

"The rabbit?" questioned Makow, amazed by the beauty of the night sky and the many falling stars. "Why are falling stars the work of a rabbit?"

Grandfather smiled, crossed his arms around himself and drew near to the fire to keep warm. "You see, Makow, how the great heaven weaves patterns with stars like fine quill work on the robe of night? Even the old stars that fall to Mother Earth make a design in the night. Well, the rabbit is the one who wove the designs in the sky first, long ago. He made it in his anger against the sun."

Makow had heard many stories all his life, especially around his grandfather's winter fires. But on this trip Grandfather seemed to have new ones to tell. The great rock and the crows must have been very busy with their stories, Makow thought. Then he urged the old man to tell this new story. "If the rabbit made all these stars with his anger, he must have been very mad."

"Oh yes. You see, the rabbit at one time was very tall and had long straight legs like yours. He even had a long tail that hung nearly to the ground. He loved to run and hunt and was very beautiful and graceful in his movements. He was very proud of the way he looked, but his pride was his downfall.

"One day, the beautiful rabbit with his long straight legs lay down on the bright shore in the soft white sand and fell into a deep sleep. He thought the warm sun, which was much larger than it is today, was his friend, and he slept as soundly as a puppy in a heap of skins.

"It wasn't until rabbit woke up that he discovered the sun had tricked him. It had burned so brightly that it made his legs shrink and bend in the heat. When rabbit tried to stand, he discovered the sun had burned off his tail, too. He now had only a little fluffy ball.

"When the rabbit finally managed to stand, he discovered he could only jump and hop, since the white sand was so hot. But each time he jumped and hopped, his legs bent even more, until jumping and hopping was all he could do. Rabbit was now very angry at the sun.

"You see, at that time the rabbit carried a small doeskin pouch full of magic pellets the size of shells. He threw these pellets at his enemies to destroy them, and it was because of them that he was such a great hunter and ate meat.

"And so the rabbit decided to take revenge against the sun. He jumped on his poor, shrunken, bent legs to the end of Mother Earth to the west, where the sun came daily to take its rest. That evening, when the sun arrived, the rabbit, in his great anger, threw all his magic pellets at the sun."

Makow started to laugh. "The magic pellets remind me of your bag of teeth, Grandfather. Perhaps you are right in saving them. Perhaps they are magic."

Grandfather smiled. "My teeth are magic, Makow, because for many snows they chewed my food for me. Now they remind me of all the good food I have eaten and will never eat again."

Makow smiled and nodded at his wisdom.

Lame Beaver continued. "The magic pellets that the rabbit threw struck the sun right in the face. They were so powerful they caused the sun to burst, like a cracked rock explodes in a hot fire.

"A piece of the great sun flew high into the blue sky and made the moon. The shower of sparks that flew into the air from the magic pellets became the stars that burn brightly in the night."

"Those pellets must have been very powerful magic as there are more stars than there are counting sticks," commented Makow as he watched the meteor shower. "So is that why the rabbit no longer eats meat? Is it because he used all his pellets on the sun?"

"Yes," agreed Grandfather. "This is what I have been told. It is also why you see the rabbit lying in the shade of bushes when he rests. He now hides from the bright hot sun."

Makow thought about how he always laid snares for rabbits in the shadows of bushes. Now he knew why.

In the protection of the canoe and the warmth of the fire, Makow finally fell asleep. He was glad that the rabbit no longer had such powerful magic, and that he and Grandfather had the light of the moon and the sparks of stars to keep them company that night. He was also glad Grandfather had not lost his bag of teeth to the waves of the lake.

## Chapter Fourteen

# FISHING

The next morning, Grandfather woke Makow early. After they put on their moccasins, they walked deep in the shadows of the woods to find the things they would need to repair the canoe.

With the long, sharp hunting knife he had captured from his enemy so long ago, Lame Beaver made thin cuts in a pine tree and removed a large square of its skin. He bent it until he had formed a container and then slit another pine to gather its gum. Not far away, the two found the spruce tree that gave them the roots they would need in case they had to sew the tear in the canoe.

The last thing they needed was harder to find. They walked a long way from the shore until, with the help of the morning sun, they discovered a white birch tree shining bright like no other tree in the forest.

Not having any kinnikinnick that was dry, Grandfather cut a piece of his long gray hair and placed it at the base of the tree. Then he looked at Makow's cut and twisted hair, smiled, and instructed him to take his crow feather and place it there as an offering.

"In nature, you must give back if you take, especially from this great old tree. Be mindful to take only what you need, because you must give back equally. Man must live with all forms of life, keeping us in balance. We must keep the great circle of life large and always growing."

Sadly, Makow pulled the crow feather out of his tangled hair and placed it at the base of the tree with Grandfather's hair.

"Makow, also remember, always give with a joyful heart. It is the right thing to do."

Makow nodded. He knew Grandfather was right.

Lame Beaver then cut a large square of bark from the tree. It was not so large or deep that the tree would not heal, but large enough to mend the canoe and have some skin to spare. The light pink inside of the birch bark quickly began to dry and redden.

"If this had been my canoe," commented Grandfather as they made their way back to camp, "I would have kept my mending supplies inside it. The canoe probably belonged to an old warrior who traveled only the short distance from his camp to Fort Detroit."

"Grandfather, you said there was balance in all

things. Is that right?"

Lame Beaver agreed with Makow. "That is so."

"Well, if that is so, perhaps this is what we get for taking a canoe that is not ours."

Grandfather paused for a moment and thought.

"You are growing wise, Makow. Perhaps you are right, even though this canoe saved our lives."

When they returned to camp the wind had softened and the two built up the fire to help them in their work. They carefully warmed the gum of the tree in the soft pine container and mixed it with charcoal from the fire. Makow split the roots of the spruce and pounded them flat between two rocks so they would dry and become strong **wattape**. With the same rocks, Grandfather pounded a fishhook straight to use as an awl to sew the tear.

Checking the canoe to make sure it was dry, Lame Beaver discovered the hole was not as bad as he had thought. With Makow's help he carefully cut the jagged edges of the rip until they were smooth. Then he used a balsam branch to paint the gum and charcoal mixture around the tear and covered it with the birch bark patch. As he carefully added more gum, lumps of pitch, blackened by the charcoal, oozed out around the seam. Spitting on his fingers, Grandfather rubbed the gum around the patch, to seal it.

"There is no need to sew with the spruce root," Grandfather explained and then covered the seam with another layer of gum. He did the same between the ribs inside the canoe.

When they were finished, Makow placed a piece of pine skin over the gum container to keep it clean. Then he wrapped the unused wattape tightly around the rest of the birch bark in a roll.

Grandfather smiled, happy with their work. "We will keep this extra with us, in case the sun hides another rock from your eyes."

Makow frowned. He had saved them from many rocks on their journey. Why not this one? Still, he knew warriors needed to know how to care for their canoes, and often had to repair them. He was glad to have his grandfather teach him these skills.

Running his hands through the sand, Lame Beaver worked the sticky gum from his fingers until they were clean. Although the sun shone brightly, there was a cool breeze that made him think of his blanket. Turning to the branches of the great pine, he was happy to discover his red English blanket had finally dried. He pulled it out of the branches carefully and wrapped it around himself, then sat contentedly in the warm sand as if he had just found an old friend.

"We are only a half sun's paddle from the fort of

the English and another from Wa-gaw-naw-ke-zee. Perhaps at the fort we will hear word of Detroit and Bwondiac," said Grandfather.

Perhaps, thought Makow, someone will also know of his mother.

Grandfather nudged Makow and pointed at the food bag that lay nearby, still damp from the day before. The white bread had been finished days before, and now the little food that was left was turning bad.

"I think we should stay here another night," said Grandfather.

Makow was surprised to hear this.

The old man continued, "Another night will allow the patch to set fully, even though I know it would be safe to travel on. Perhaps, Makow, you could find fish in the river that we can cook for our evening meal."

Makow brightened, since fishing always sounded like a good idea to him.

"If you follow the lakeshore, you will find the mouth of the river. Do not be long, but bring back many big fish," Grandfather said smiling. "I will see what else I can find in the woods for us to eat."

Makow stood and brushed the sand from his legs. He would need the fishing ball with its leather string and fishhooks. As he searched through his pouch, he noticed his grandfather, wrapped in his English blanket, had stretched out in the shadow of the canoe for a rest.

Makow followed the shore until he came to the wide mouth and high banks of the Cheboygan. Makow made his way along the bank and around a curve in the river, where he discovered a quiet place with patches of sunlight glistening on the slow-moving water. There, a low branch of a large, leafy tree reached out over the face of the river.

After climbing out onto the limb and stretching himself out on its rough bark, Makow lowered his string with its barbed hook into the water and waited. It was not long before he heard the beating of wings above his head. Makow looked up to see a great, black crow landing on the tree branch above him. The bird gave a loud caw and flapped its wings.

Makow wondered what story the crow wanted to tell him. The fishing was hopeless with the crow's loud voice and its flapping wings that cast shadows across the water. Makow pulled his fishing string from the water, rolled it back into a ball, and carefully edged his way off the branch to the riverbank.

Makow watched and listened as the bird continued to call out. What did he want?

Laying his fishing string aside, Makow waved his arms wildly, trying to scare the noisy bird away. But the crow wouldn't leave. Determined not to leave his fishing spot, Makow climbed back up the tree, this time working his way up toward the crow. He grabbed the branch the crow was on and shook it.

The crow turned to Makow as if smiling and flew away. Just then, Makow caught sight of two canoes coming down the river. As they approached he could see they were filled with warriors with their faces painted red and black, as if it were time to make battle.

They are not Odawa, thought Makow. Their paint designs and hair were different from his people. He decided they were Ojibwa who lived on Minissing Mackinac.

Makow pressed close to the trunk of the tree, trying to hide himself in the leaves. The canoes, carrying three men each, quickly glided beneath him.

As he looked down on their painted heads and strong bare backs, Makow wondered if these were some of Bwondiac's men. *Grandfather!* thought Makow. Would these warriors see his grandfather sleeping beneath the canoe when they reached the lake? Makow hoped the warriors would turn west towards the English fort and not pass the spot where he and Grandfather camped.

At that moment the great black crow flew straight

at Makow, shrieking and beating his wings wildly. Trying to shield his face from the bird, Makow slipped and slid against the rough bark of the tree trunk. Below him the warriors turned quickly and shouted, pointing to Makow, who had grabbed the branch where he once fished and now dangled helplessly. Directing their canoes ashore, the warriors leapt onto the bank and ran to the tree. The crow, squawking and beating his wings, continued to betray Makow. Gathered below, the warriors called and motioned for Makow to come down. Terrified, Makow continued to hold onto the branch. A warrior reached up, grabbing and pulling Makow by his moccasin.

The men laughed and threw small stones at him. Finally Makow decided he had no choice. He began to work his way along the branch toward the tree's trunk so he could crawl down. The warrior who held Makow's moccasin let go, but another grabbed him by the leg and yanked him to the ground.

Makow lay flat on his back and tried to catch his breath as the warriors surrounded him and spoke loudly in a language he did not understand. Now he knew they were not Ojibwa, as the Ojibwa spoke a language similar to the Odawa's.

Frightened, Makow tried to get up, but one of the men put his foot on Makow's chest and pushed him back down. They all laughed as they bullied him. Makow again tried to stand, but it was impossible because they leaned over him like a pack of wolves.

The crow who had created Makow's dilemma gave one last caw, fluttered his wings, and finally flew away. Makow was afraid for his life. These warriors were not like his people.

The group of warriors laughed at Makow and said many things he did not understand. Makow tried again to escape, pitching himself into the water to try to swim away. As he fought to swim to the opposite shore, Makow heard the warriors splashing behind him. Soon a great hand reached out and grabbed him by his chopped hair. Angrily the warrior shook Makow and dragged him toward shore. Makow kicked and fought, but it was useless.

Just then the blast of a flintlock rifle echoed along the river. The warriors jumped in surprise and dashed toward their canoe, dragging Makow with them. Makow fought like he had never fought before until he managed to free himself. Exhausted, he dropped into the water, away from their reach, and again tried to swim away.

As a warrior reached out to grab Makow again, another blast from the flintlock changed his mind. This time the enemy stopped and ran as fast as he could toward the canoes that were already escaping.

Makow quickly hid himself along the water's edge as the sound from the warriors' canoe blades splashed away. Makow could now see the thick gray smoke from the gunpowder blast floating on the breeze above the river. From the swirling haze, there now emerged the outline of a big, redheaded man standing tall in the bow of a canoe.

## Chapter Fifteen

# ENEMIES

The warriors' angry war-whoops echoed through the woods as they disappeared toward the mouth of the river. Not wanting to meet another stranger, Makow stayed in the water crouched among the reeds and cattails. But they did not hide him.

"A-hoy thar," called the red-haired man as he splashed from the canoe, its bow painted with the design of a peace pipe. "I'll not hurt ya. Ya be all right?"

His was like the voice of the Scottish traders Makow had heard near Fort Detroit. Makow, afraid of what might happen, sprung from the water and ran, again, to the safety of the tree.

"Boy, stop!" the big man ordered.

Makow climbed a few feet up into the arms of the tree before the man caught him by the foot and brought him, once again, tumbling to the ground. As Makow lay on the ground, he could see above him the great black crow returning to his perch to watch Makow's capture. A crow will never be painted on my drum, thought Makow angrily.

Then Makow heard another person coming ashore from the canoe. A laughing voice approached and said, "Da, what did ya catch? He looks like a wild wolf. Look at his raggedy hair stickin' out all over."

Now Makow could see this one was not a man, but a boy his own age.

As the large red-haired man peered down at Makow, he began to speak in what sounded like the same language the warriors had spoken. Makow was frightened.

"He be not Sauk," said the man to the boy. He doesn't understand what I'm sayin'."

Next the man tried the language spoken by the Odawa. "Aanii (Hello)," he said, reaching out his great bear paw of a hand to help Makow to his feet.

Makow pushed the man's hand away and stood up without his help. In a flash Makow turned and pushed the boy aside with all his might, and began to run away.

The boy fell and rolled toward the river, but in a few leaps the man caught Makow's arm.

"Ya be a fast runner, boy. Good long legs!"

Makow squirmed but could not pull free from the man's bear-like grasp.

"Mark, ya be all right?" The boy, now covered with dirt and mud, stood and glared at Makow. "Are ya all right?" questioned the man again.

"Aye, I be fine, but this wild one needs to be taught a lesson, don't ya think, Da?" The boy tried to brush the dirt from his cloth pants and straightened himself.

"I think this one's had enough for the day. He's nothing but afraid." The man eased his grip on Makow's arm and looked him in the eye.

"What are ya doing here alone? Don't ya know there is danger in the woods now?" Makow stared straight ahead and did not answer.

The boy now approached Makow. "Do ya hear what he asks? Answer him!" he demanded. The boy's dark eyes flashed with anger.

Makow wiggled loose from the man's grip and lunged at the boy. But before he could reach him, the boy pulled back his fist and hit Makow in the nose.

Makow jumped on the boy and they both rolled together down the bank into the water. They wrestled with the water splashing around them until the man pulled them from the water by their arms and shook them both.

"Ya not be doing this, ya hear? Mark, ya be mean for no reason. Yar blood is too hot. Settle yourself," demanded the red-haired man.

With anger in his eyes, the boy called Mark balled

up his fist again, but Makow had had enough and covered his face with his arms. Though the boy was shorter, Makow knew he had the heart of an enemy and would hurt him. He was not like any of the Scottish traders Makow knew from Fort Detroit. This boy, Makow thought, was not to be trusted.

Mark pulled away, and leaning over into the water, washed the mud and leaves from his face. Untying the ribbon that held the **queue** of his long black hair, he smoothed it flat and tied it again close to his head.

"Now, I don't know what to do with ya," said the man as he held Makow, who was dripping with water and mud. "I suppose we can take ya to the fort."

"Leave him in the woods, Da. Perhaps more Sauks will find him," offered Mark.

"No more talk till yar blood cools, ya hear?" demanded the man.

The boy stomped back to their canoe and stood waiting. Just then Makow heard the voice of his grandfather calling out, "**Bozhoo**! Aanii!"

The red-haired man straightened, and Mark dove for the rifle in the bow of the canoe.

"Grandfather!" hollered Makow.

"Makow, what have you been up to?" asked Grandfather with a smile, as he limped out of the woods. It was the same smile Makow had often seen him use when trading with the English at Detroit.

"What troubles have you found yourself in?" He gave Makow a look that said he was to stay quiet.

Grandfather offered his arm to the red-haired man, who offered his arm back. The great hand of the man nearly surrounded Grandfather's elbow in the exchange.

"Bozhoo. I'm MacGinity, from Montreal. Thar is me boy, Mark."

"I am Lame Beaver. As you can see." Grandfather bounced a little on his lame leg, and the two men began to laugh.

"Aye, I can see. And this be yours?" MacGinity asked, releasing his hold on Makow.

"Makow, my grandson."

Makow looked down, unwilling to make friends with either this red-haired bear or his boy.

"Makow," snapped Grandfather, demanding respect for the strangers. Makow looked up and smiled.

"The boy had a scare a wee bit ago," continued MacGinity. "The Sauk had him and were going to make sport of him. It was lucky we came along when we did."

Grandfather's eyes grew big when he heard what had happened to Makow. "I am grateful to you and your son. Our camp is to the east of the mouth of the river. We stopped to repair our canoe. When I went into the woods to find roots to boil for our meal, I heard the thunder of your flintlock. Perhaps I am just an old dog worrying about his pup, but that is why I came." Grandfather laughed and so did the red-haired man.

"He was sent to fish, I did not know he would catch Sauk. Why do the Sauk visit here from across the river of the Illinois?" asked Lame Beaver, concerned.

"I do not know. Along the route from Montreal we heard stories of Chief Bwondiac trying to stir things up. I have heard from the Indians I just traded with that he has now gotten help all the way from the Mississippi to the Atlantic. It appears the French are in on it, telling Bwondiac they'll return and take back the land. They say the Indians who help them will receive gifts."

"Is that true?" asked Grandfather. "Will the French return?"

"The French are a bunch of cowards!" interrupted Mark, joining the group. "Cowards, the lot of them! They ran from Montreal and they ran from Quebec. They don't even own property here. It belongs to us now."

Makow's eyes narrowed angrily as this boy insulted his father's people.

"What's wrong?" snapped Mark at Makow. "Could it be ya have some French in ya? You don't look like other Indians with yar wild, bushy hair."

"Mark! Mind yar manners," snapped MacGinity. "Ya have to excuse me boy. He has been with voyageurs too long in the wilderness. I raised him meself from just a wee one. We be always on the move without the taming effects of a mother."

Lame Beaver reached out his hand and gently placed it on the boy's shoulder, much to Makow's distress. "I, too, understand how it is to raise a boy. I helped raise Makow after his brave French father died riding the great falls of Niagara."

Mark stared at Lame Beaver. How could anyone ride the great falls of Niagara, he wondered.

"If the boy's father tried to ride Niagara, he is a braver man than meself," said MacGinity. "I have seen its power and heard its thunder."

Mark walked away and stood silently. "Ride the falls," he said under his breath. "It has to be a wild Indian story."

Curious about Detroit, Lame Beaver pressed MacGinity for more news. "Bwondiac—does he push forward with his Beaver War?"

"Beaver War? I never heard it called by that name.

It's more the war of Amherst, who is now in charge. The trouble isn't all with Bwondiac. Amherst has warned all the traders not to trade gunpowder or weapons to any of the Indians. And he gives no gifts for the use of their land.

"This Englishman doesn't know the mind of the Indian, only the mind of the English," continued MacGinity. "He tries to look good to King George and save him gold and silver that he will put in his own purse when he returns home. He cares not about the people here.

"If Amherst were a wise man," added MacGinity, "he would pave an even broader road of friendship, one that would stretch to the setting sun."

"Da, ya shouldn't be saying words like that," scolded Mark.

"Bad decisions spread themselves among many nations," said MacGinity to his son, and then continued his discussion with Lame Beaver.

"Amherst refuses to give gifts because he has said it is like rewarding bad children when they do not do what they are told. So all Indians as well as the traders suffer."

"This war that Amherst has started will cause many to go hungry," said Lame Beaver. "The corn and all the rest of our harvest, this season and last, has been bad for lack of rain. Without gunpowder to hunt with, our people will go hungry."

"Aye, and without gunpowder, the trade will dry up. That is what scares me. That is why I thought I would take me boy farther west to Rainy Lake and leave this place forever.

"So if ya know nothing of Amherst or Bwondiac, Lame Beaver, what are ya doing out here? Where ya be headin'?" questioned MacGinity.

Makow glanced up at Grandfather, wondering how he would answer. "I take the boy to Wa-gaw-naw-ke-zee, Bent Tree. We are Odawa. It is his time of seeking. We have been upon the water for many suns and do not want trouble."

"Aye, ya be right, old Lame Beaver. Stay as far from trouble as ya can. Peace is always better. That is why I painted the design of the peace pipe on the bow of me canoe."

Makow was surprised to hear the words of his mother coming from the red bear. *Peace is better.* Makow thought on those words. He looked over to the canoe where Mark stood and met his gaze with an icy stare. This boy, Makow knew, had a great warrior inside, although he was small in stature. But he had not yet learned MacGinity's lesson of peace.

"I know Bent Tree," MacGinity went on. "I was

there a few seasons back making trade. Big village, lodges as far as the eye can see, and Odawa."

"It was once my home. That is why we return. It is the place where I went many snows ago, when I walked straight and still had my teeth." Grandfather and MacGinity laughed together. Makow smiled. He liked MacGinity.

"Seeking? What's that?" asked Mark as he joined in the conversation.

"It is when a young warrior goes to the woods to wait for answers to come to our questions. Answers that will help us in our lives," answered Lame Beaver.

"Sit in the woods and wait fer answers? To what questions?" asked Mark.

"This is how an Indian boy grows up. It is the Indian way," interrupted MacGinity.

"But the Indian way is over, just like the French way is over. And it's wrong. Now it's time to believe the right things. It's our territory now," said Mark.

Grandfather looked at MacGinity, not knowing what to say to such a disrespectful boy as this.

"French, Indian, English or Scottish, it is only a person who can be wrong—wrong when he does wrong," insisted MacGinity. "Just because we are different, doesn't mean we are wrong or right. We see through different eyes, and we must respect these eyes. It is a lesson that is hard to learn."

"A-ho, MacGinity, you are a wise man," said Grandfather. I hope you make money in the trade if you teach those words to all people."

"So, ya say yar canoe is damaged?" asked MacGinity, trying to turn the subject away from his son's disrespectful remarks. "Do ya need us to take ya to the fort?"

"There's no room in our canoe!" snapped Mark.

"Then you'll be making room," returned his father. Mark shook his head in disgust.

"Miig-wech, MacGinity. You are a good man, but our canoe is repaired. We only have need of food."

"Now that I can be a help with. Would ya have anything ta trade for it?" asked MacGinity with a smile. "Mark, bring our food sack."

The boy looked up at his father in surprise. "Hurry, lad, we will be at the fort this evening and can eat from our larder there.

"I have nothing to trade. We are poor Odawa and all we had was spoiled by the lake."

Makow watched as Mark slowly pulled back the oilcloth that covered their supplies.

"Mark!" snapped MacGinity. "Hurry, lad!

"Well, Lame Beaver, since you have nothing to

trade, I will take yar friendship and that of yar grandson. Ya have to promise to stop by the fort on yar way to Bent Tree."

"Yes, MacGinity," smiled Grandfather. "This I have to trade and promise. We will be brothers of the trail, if not of our blood." He reached out his arm to his new red-haired friend.

Mark brought the food bag to his father and stood waiting for instructions.

"Hand it to them, lad."

"All of it?" Mark questioned.

"Aye, don't be stingy. We have eaten plenty this day. Lame Beaver and Makow are probably hungry after all the excitement. Especially Makow.

"Lame Beaver, ya would have been proud of yar grandson. If we had not come along, I am sure he would soon have had all those Sauk down on the ground, or perhaps he would have run them into the lake with those long legs of his. Right Mark?"

Mark looked up at his tall father. He held out the bag to Lame Beaver.

"My arms are stiff because I am an old, lame Indian. I don't know if I am strong enough to carry such a heavy bag of food from my friend MacGinity and his boy. Makow will carry the bag, as he is strong."

Mark turned to Makow and rolled his eyes, holding out the heavy bag.

"You have been very kind in saving Makow and giving us food," added Lame Beaver.

"Remember, ya owe us a visit at the fort. Can we take ya to yar canoe?" offered MacGinity.

Lame Beaver looked at Mark, who hoped they would refuse. "Your father is a good man. I hope you grow to be like him. Makow and I can find our way back through the woods, Miig-wech.

"Makow...." Grandfather nodded his head toward his grandson, and Makow understood what he was to do.

"Miig-wech, MacGinity," said Makow as he offered his arm. "Thank you for scaring away the Sauk and for the food." The two shook arms. Then Grandfather nudged Makow with his elbow, and Makow put down the food sack and walked to Mark.

"Miig-wech, Mark." Makow offered his arm and Mark turned away.

"Mark!" snapped MacGinity. "Shake with our new friend."

Mark turned reluctantly and offered his arm.

MacGinity and Mark waded out into the water, pushed their canoe away from the shore, and disappeared around the bend in the river toward the great lake.

## Chapter Sixteen

# NAMES

Lame Beaver and Makow made their way back along the riverbank and through the forest toward their camp. It was then Makow remembered his leather string and fishhooks, lost in the struggle with the Sauks.

"Wait, Grandfather!" he called and bounded back to the place where he had tried to fish. On the branch above him, he heard movement in the leaves. It was the crow again.

"Go away! You are not my friend anymore," yelled Makow.

The bird called out to him in a loud caw.

"Go away!" yelled Makow again, swinging his arms above his head. Just then he spied his ball of leather string and fish hooks, hanging from a tree branch. How did it get up there, he wondered.

The crow called out to him again, as if answering his question. Makow shook his head and asked the crow,"So why is it you help me now?" He reached up and snapped the tiny branch that held the line and caught it as it fell. Winding it up and pulling the leaves and twigs from it, Makow looked up as the bird flew away.

Rejoining his grandfather, Makow picked up the food sack and the two resumed their walk back to the Lake of the Hurons.

As Lame Beaver walked, he thought about the boy Mark and his own grandson. "Makow, I am happy you are my grandson," he said. "It would be hard to find a place in my heart for a grandson like that boy Mark. It would take much work to teach him respect. He has many hard lessons to learn."

Makow smiled, happy to have a grandfather like Lame Beaver to teach him.

As they approached the shore of the lake, Lame Beaver stopped. Before they stepped into the open, he peered through the pines to see if all was safe.

Once in camp, Lame Beaver checked the canoe to make sure the patch had taken so that they could leave early the next morning. Makow sat down near the small glowing pile of ash that had been their fire and opened the food sack. Food was the most important thing on his mind, and he was delighted to discover a bag of smoked venison and a small loaf of the white English bread.

Grandfather smiled at the treat. "There are only

two things English I like, white bread and MacGinity."

"Three," interrupted Makow. "You also like English blankets." Makow smiled at Lame Beaver as he pulled his warm, red English blanket snug around his shoulders.

"Yes, you are right, Grandson. Now there are three English things I like."

As Makow chewed on venison, he fed bits and pieces of wood to the ashes and rekindled a small flame. Then he placed their dried mats and blankets in the shelter of the mended canoe so that they could sit near the fire and feast on the contents of the food bag.

Lame Beaver broke off a chunk of the crusty white bread and popped it into his mouth, savoring its taste. "White bread to the English," he said, "is like corn and wild rice to our people. It is most important and very good."

"It was also good MacGinity came along when he did. If the Sauk are here wearing the paint of war because of Bwondiac, they will want to make trouble. You might just be the type of trouble they would think was fun."

"MacGinity, he is good for a Scotsman—or an Englishman," said Makow as he ripped off a piece of bread and chewed it.

Grandfather smiled. "That is true, but don't say that to MacGinity. I have heard from traders around Detroit that the Scots are not true friends of the English. They are another nation of people, like Iroquois and Odawa. They live close to each other and share many things, but they do not share a fondness for each other.

"It is the same with the French and English," Grandfather explained. "The French came to our land to live and are our friends. The English, too, came from across the great sea but have never been friends with the French, and only a few Indians. That's also true with many Scots, but not MacGinity, who has traded for our friendship."

"It is hard to understand," said Makow, "how these white men look much the same but can be so different. And how can the boy Mark be so different from MacGinity, his own blood?"

"The boy is young and MacGinity will continue to teach him. Perhaps some day he will learn and become a great friend and trader to our people."

Makow shook his head in disbelief. "There is much for him to learn. MacGinity should take him for a time of seeking.

Grandfather smiled and agreed. "A time of seeking for this boy would change his heart forever. I was told by my grandfather when I was very young that Indians were like the rocks, upon this land forever. The Europeans are like the water, blown upon us by a heavy storm and creating a flood.

"The rock is hard and strong and holds its ground, but the water can gradually wear away the rock. Sometimes the water even breaks the rock and the rock becomes many small stones.

"But I was also told," continued Lame Beaver, "to remember that the rock endures, whether it is a strong mountain or grains of sand. And we should always remember that we are rocks upon this land and forever part of Mother Earth."

Makow smiled. "Your grandfather, my great-great-grandfather, was a wise man."

"He was a good teacher, too," added Lame Beaver as he gummed his English bread.

"Grandfather, this flood of people from across the great sea, do they look alike to you?" Makow asked seriously.

"It is true. They all wear the same clothes and eat the same food," answered his grandfather.

"But how do they know who is their friend and who is not?" asked Makow. "Our Three Fires, we are different people. We paint our faces and make our tattoo differently. We cut our hair and make our quill and bead work differently. The food we eat is not the same.

"The Odawa hunt much and raise few crops," Makow continued, "trading often with the French and now the English. The Ojibwa are hunting people who trade little, and the Potawatomi plant crops and raise much corn. We are all very different.

"We know what our enemies look like and who our friends are. But this is not true for the people from across the sea. How do they know whom to trust? And how do we know now that they live among us?"

"This is a good question, Makow," said Lame Beaver.

Makow continued, "It is like that boy Mark. I know he is my enemy in all the things he says and does. There is no mistake. I must be careful of him. But MacGinity is now our friend. And what of my own brother? You say I will know him when we meet. You said my brother was taken by the English in a raid, and Mother said she heard of an Odawa boy living with a trader. If I did not truly trust my heart, I might have mistaken this enemy for my brother."

Lame Beaver nodded. "These things you say are true, Makow. It would be a hard thing to understand if your brother was your enemy. It would be like a great trick played upon you."

"Like the trick the crow played this day," complained Makow. "The crow I do not understand either. I think he has now learned to take stories from us two-legged humans and needed a new one to tell on the wind, and I am now that story. I do not think the crow is my friend anymore."

"Friends are sometimes hard to understand. They do many things differently than you, but may still have you in their heart."

Makow thought of his mother and nodded. "You are right, Grandfather, many things are hard to understand. But will you now tell me about my name and about my brother? Tell me also how I will know him, so I will not mistake an enemy for my own blood."

Clearing his throat and pointing to the islands across the straits, Lame Beaver began, "Can you see the three islands, Makow?"

Makow nodded but then lowered his head in disappointment, as it seemed it was not yet time for his questions to be answered.

"The large one is called Bois Blanc, a French name meaning white wood. They named it for the birch trees that grow there. The next is called Round Island, named by the English, because of its shape. The third is called Michilimackinac, named by our people. Do you know why we named it that?"

Makow nodded. "Yes, I have been told. It comes from *mi-she*, which means large, and *mi-ki-nock*, which is the name for the mud turtle. It is named 'great turtle' because of its shape."

"So that is what you have heard about the name. Did you know a name can mean more than what you understand it to mean?" Lame Beaver asked.

Makow scrunched up his face and wondered what Grandfather meant.

"You see there is another reason for that name. This I know, as I was told the story by my grandfather before I was as big as you. He told me that before the European came, even before the Odawa lived at Bent Tree, there was a small nation of people that lived upon that island of the Great Turtle, and their names were the Mi-shi-ne-macki-naw-go.

"The Mi-shi-ne-macki-naw-go became friends with our nation, the Odawa, when we lived near them on the islands the Hurons now call Manitoulin in Georgian Bay. We called those islands the Odawa Islands, many lifetimes ago.

"The small nation that lived on the island of the Great Turtle was very weak and became an easy target for the Iroquois, who wished to control the beaver trade as far as the sun sets. The Iroquois came to the island, destroyed this nation, and moved on to fight with the Ojibwa at the rapids of Ba-weting (Sault Ste. Marie).

"When our people discovered the Mi-shi-ne-macki-naw-go were no more, we blackened our faces with soot and cried the death song for them. It was then our people began calling the island, Mi-shi-ne-macki-nong, in honor of those who lost their lives at the hands of our enemy.

"So you see," Grandfather concluded, "names mean many things to many people. And perhaps, what you think a name means is not always all of the story."

Makow looked at his grandfather and thought about the small nation upon the island and how they were lost. And now, even the story of the name had been lost to those who knew a different story. It made Makow sad to think how easy it was to forget and how hard it is to remember.

"Makow, it was that way with you and your brother. You came onto Mother Earth together, but you and your brother were very different."

Makow listened closely and watched as Grandfather fed the fire with another stick of wood and pulled his English blanket snug around his shoulders. The shadows of night closed in around them as the waves of the Lake of the Hurons washed one upon the other onto the shore.

"I have heard you many times," continued Lame Beaver, "question the meaning of your own name."

Makow agreed. "Bear Skin is a funny name. Each time I tried to guess its meaning, both you and Mother laughed but wouldn't tell me."

"That is true. Makow, look upon my shoulder. What do you see here?"

Makow reached over and pulled his grandfather's red blanket away from his shoulder, revealing on the old warrior's sagging skin a faded design placed there many snows before.

"It is a design, Grandfather."

"That is true. But it is also a symbol of remembrance, pricked into my skin by your mother's needle and rubbed with soot, so we would never forget."

"Forget what?" asked Makow. "The design is like the one mother made on the sheath of my knife. It is the mark of two bear claws."

"That is so. But our totem is the crane, not the bear. Why would your mother make the sign of the bear claw?"

Makow thought hard. "Perhaps, Grandfather, it was to remind you that you were once a warrior like the mighty bear?"

Grandfather smiled and ran his tongue over his broken teeth. "I was not so strong as a great bear,

Makow."

"The bear is the medicine animal. Was it good medicine, to keep you strong?"

"It is not that reason either, Makow. Your name, Makowaian or Bear Skin, has a meaning like kinnikinnick, which means 'much mixed.' It is like the island of Michilimackinac and like the symbol on my shoulder. It is a much-mixed name to remind you of the bear, but also to remind your mother you were the son whose skin was bare, with no spots from the time of your birth."

"What does that mean, Grandfather? What does all of this mean?"

Grandfather peered into the fire that had again started to burn low. "Makow, you now know the meaning of your name, and this day has been hard. I want you to sleep upon this meaning."

"Will you not tell me more this night?"

"No, Makow. It is time for you to dream upon these things."

The old man lay back on his mat and pulled his blanket up around him to keep out the cool night.

Makow sat silently, puzzled by the riddle his grandfather had left him. How could he dream for an answer, when the question kept sleep so far away from him?

## Chapter Seventeen

# MICHILIMACKINAC

The next morning the glowing red sun burned at Makow's eyes and awakened him. Makow did not feel rested, since his sleep had been interrupted many times by his grandfather's riddle. Makow lifted himself onto his elbow and shaded his eyes. His grandfather's sleep mat was already rolled tightly, and a fire crackled with dry pine branches.

Makow spotted Grandfather standing near the shore. The old man had gathered his turtle pouch, MacGinity's food bag, and the canoe repair kit, and Makow knew it would soon be time to leave. Lame Beaver motioned to him to join him near the shore.

"Gisis (Sun) gives us a good morning to travel to the fort of the English," Lame Beaver commented. "We will visit our friend MacGinity and your friend Mark."

Makow tried to ignore his grandfather's comment as he reached into the food bag for a chunk of white bread and a few pieces of dried meat.

"I am worried to hear the Sauk are gathering from

the rivers of the Ouisconsin and Fox," said Lame Beaver. "That is a long paddle, past La Baye (Green Bay). It would take a great plan for them to travel this far, perhaps a plan of Bwondiac's.

"The fort we visit this day is a very important place," he continued. "It is the place that connects all the routes to the upper countries of the Great Lakes to the Mississippi, and to the northwest, where MacGinity will travel. It is a place of importance for the English, and because of that, it will be a place of importance for Bwondiac.

"We must keep our eyes sharp today to avoid danger. If I had not promised to visit MacGinity, we would pass by the fort and continue to Wa-gaw-naw-ke-zee. So we will make a short visit with MacGinity and be on our way."

Makow understood Grandfather's concern. He did not wish to visit the Sauk he had met upon the river the day before. As he ate his bread and venison, Makow used his bare toes to trace the outline of a rock that lay just beneath the sand. When he finished his venison, he stooped down and scooped the wet sand away, revealing a round, spotted rock. Unlike my name, this has many spots, Makow thought as he held it up for Lame Beaver to inspect.

"It has a design," said Lame Beaver. "This is good."

Together they carried the canoe to the water. Lame Beaver waded beside the canoe, all the while watching the patch to make sure it held tight and no water leaked in around the hardened gum. When he was satisfied the repair was holding, Lame Beaver guided the fragile vessel near shore and Makow began loading it, putting his sweat lodge rocks in the center to give it weight and balance.

When they finished, Grandfather hopped in and Makow waded the canoe out until the green water reached his stomach and they were well away from the dangerous rocks. Then he carefully pulled himself up and into the vessel. He nodded to his grandfather and they began their westward journey toward Fort Michilimackinac.

The two soon passed the mouth of the river Cheboygan. Lame Beaver nudged Makow with his long paddle and pointed. There near the river's mouth on a naked branch of a windblown tree sat a large black crow, flapping its wings in the breeze.

Grandfather laughed, "It sends you on your way."

"It can leave me alone and be on its own way," replied Makow, ignoring the crow and continuing to paddle.

Later, Makow watched with great interest as they passed the islands of Bois Blanc and Round. Then came Minissing Michilimackinac, named in memory of the people who once lived there. Makow studied its white cliffs bleached by the sun. Beyond the island and across the straits Makow could soon see a point of land in the distance, a place Grandfather called the old Mission of St. Ignacious. Trees hanging with moss and broken branches walled the water's edge. Above them screeching gulls circled the water, one by one plunging into the lake to fish for food. Ducks and cormorants passed overhead.

Lame Beaver now directed the canoe toward the southern shore. Makow was glad there was only a light breeze as they began to cross the open water. As the shore began to take form, he spotted trails of gray smoke drifting into the air. Soon he could see the flag of the English fluttering in the wind above the tops of a picketed wall. It was Fort Michilimackinac.

Makow watched as the gray wooden walls of the palisade grew closer and closer. He began to see the lodges that lined the shoreline. Canoes rested along a shore of sand and stones, and many Indian families walked and lounged together in the sun.

"There are many here," commented Lame Beaver. "It has been many snows since I have visited this place, but there were never this many canoes and lodges here."

Makow turned and saw the worried look upon Grandfather's face.

"We paddle on farther." Lame Beaver motioned with his paddle to continue.

As they passed the fort, Makow noticed several small houses that looked like those of the French and Canadian traders around Detroit. They were small and painted white with roofs of bark and tall fences of wooden pickets surrounding them. There, too, were many canoes turned upside down upon the beach.

Now that they had surveyed the settlement Lame Beaver brought the canoe back around to a wide gate in the fort wall, where the pickets stood nearly in the water. Then he lay his paddle on the floor of the canoe and eased himself into the cool water of the lake. Makow joined him and together they waded the canoe to shore being careful to avoid rocks. Once ashore they carefully lifted the canoe on the stones and soft sand.

"You can't leave your canoe there," shouted a young English soldier from his post near the opening of the water gate.

Lame Beaver looked up in surprise to hear the voice of such a young man coming from someone wearing the red coat of a soldier.

"Hear me, old man? You can't leave the canoe so

close to the gate. Carry it down to where the Indians are making camp, unless you have trade goods to bring in."

"Miig-wech," replied Lame Beaver as he motioned for Makow to help lift the canoe back into the water. Together, they carefully guided their canoe to the edge of the palisades and again pulled it ashore. There they unloaded their belongings and placed them under the upturned canoe for safekeeping.

"I think someone has come to pay you a visit, Makow," chuckled Grandfather.

Makow turned and saw a great black crow sitting on the corner of the fort wall. The crow jerked his feathered head from side to side and cawed down at them.

"That bird brings me only bad stories," said Makow as they walked towards the gate near the water. Lame Beaver stopped. Stooping over he splashed water on his face and hair to tidy himself. Makow stopped and did the same, trying his best to flatten his hair.

Lame Beaver reached out his rough hand and tried to tame Makow's wild hair. "We must look good when we visit our friend MacGinity," he smiled. "Here, I found this." He handed Makow a black feather.

Makow looked uncertain, not sure if he should take it or not.

"You never know if an enemy is really an enemy, or just a confused friend," Grandfather reminded him.

Makow smiled and nodded, taking the sleek black feather from his grandfather's hand and placing it behind his ear.

As they neared the gate, the young guard asked them stiffly, "You have business here?"

"My friend MacGinity asked me to come see him," answered Lame Beaver.

"MacGinity? Is he back again with that boy of his? His cabin is straight through and to the right."

Lame Beaver looked puzzled at the young soldier's directions.

"That way, old man." He turned and pointed through the fort gate.

"Miig-wech, Englishman," said Lame Beaver.

## Chapter Eighteen

# MACGINITY

Inside the high wooden walls of sun-bleached pickets were many small, square houses, washed gray by the winds of the lake. The fort was filled with noise and crowded with forest runners, Indians, clerks, traders and soldiers.

Makow noticed a long cabin where there was much activity. Many young men, some in uniform, some in light work shirts, went in and out. When a man in a bright red coat with many shiny buttons approached and raised his voice to the soldiers, they stopped and stood straight.

"Major Etherington, sir!" shouted one soldier who stood tall and touched his brow with the side of his flat hand.

Lame Beaver smiled at Makow and commented, "He must be chief of the fort."

In the center of the fort, there was a wide open area where voyageurs and traders, with their red knit hats, and English soldiers, and Indians of all ages stood, talked, smoked their pipes and played games.

Makow had never been in the fort at Detroit, but this one seemed to be much larger. His grandfather pointed to an open space as they walked by. "That is the place the soldiers practice marching. They march in a line like small ducks following their mother. I saw it often when I was a boy. French and English march the same."

"Watch for MacGinity's red hair," he added. It is like a flag for us."

Makow was surprised to see the fort so full of activity. He noticed many Indians were dressed in colorful cloth with elaborate head feathers, silver earrings, and tin bells that tinkled. Some even had their faces painted. Makow realized the designs on most of their faces matched those of the Sauk he had met along the river. This was not a good thing. Even Makow knew the colors they wore were the colors of war. Makow wondered, why do the English not worry? Why do they not see? Has the great war chief Bwondiac found his way here already?

Suddenly a hand reached out and grabbed at Grandfather's red English blanket. Lame Beaver and Makow both turned quickly to pounce upon the thief, only to find MacGinity smiling at them.

"Ya be jumpy, me friend," laughed MacGinity, delighted to see them both.

"MacGinity. It was good you didn't try that in the woods. I would have had to fight you," said Lame Beaver with a chuckle, as he reached out his arm to his friend. Together they shook.

"Makow, I suppose ya seen the Sauk?"

Makow nodded.

"Not to worry. I hear they have arrived for a competition of baggataway with the Ojibwa from the island tomorrow. Supposed to be in celebration of good ol' King George's birthday. They're all harmless, I'm told.

"Well, come on. No sense standing around in the sun. Come to me shack and rest."

MacGinity led them down the gravel road to an old cabin built in the French style, with the logs of wood upright and stuck together with white clay. MacGinity released the latch and pushed the door open with his foot.

"Tisn't much, but it keeps the rain off our necks. I have rented here for the last two seasons, and I get along with Major Etherington, the boss around here, well enough. I suppose, since we leave for Rainy Lake soon, this will be the last season we will have need of it."

Inside, the smell of many years of fires filled the air, along with the grease of animal skins and the scent of English rubbish. Makow remembered the smell of the air at Detroit and wondered how it could be that the English could live so close to their own filth.

The dark cabin had a low ceiling and contained a table with two benches and two wooden chairs. There was a rope bed covered with a heavy red wool blanket, and in the corner a ladder led to the loft. Above the fireplace, MacGinity had hung several beaver traps and his flintlock. Two heavy capotes made from good English blankets hung on pegs by the door.

"Mark should be back in a bit. He is out visiting with the soldiers in the barracks. Here, Lame Beaver, sit down. Let me get ya some cider to refresh yarself. Makow, sit at the table." MacGinity pulled out the bench from the table for Makow and a large wooden chair with a soft pillow filled with balsam for Lame Beaver.

"Sit! Me home is yars," he instructed with a smile.

"Thank you, friend." Lame Beaver sat down, motioning to Makow to do the same.

MacGinity took two clay cups from a shelf and placed them on the rough wooden table. Makow watched as the bear-like man then picked up a large brown jug and pulled its stopper out with his teeth.

Lame Beaver laughed. "That is good, MacGinity.

I remember when I was able to do that," he said. "Now it is even hard to chew my food." Lame Beaver smiled showing his broken, jagged teeth.

"I know what ya mean, Lame Beaver. Last winter I had a tooth full of infection. Me mouth was so swollen, I had to do something. So I took a swig of cider and reached in and pulled what was hurting. Just yanked it right out of me head. It hurt so bad I danced and hopped about in pain and ran smack into the wall, knocking meself out. Mark found me on the floor after he returned from the trap lines and pulled me to me bed.

"The next morning, I discovered I had pulled the wrong tooth!" MacGinity opened his mouth and stuck his finger into the large gap in his gums.

Makow's eyes grew wide. Soon the red-haired bear would carry a bag of teeth like Grandfather, he thought. MacGinity poured two clay mugs of cider and brought out some white bread.

"MacGinity, you are one tough Scotsman," laughed Lame Beaver.

"Well, 'tis nice of ya to say. Some would say I was just a dumb Scotsman for that stunt."

Makow took a drink of the cider. It was sweet and tingled in his mouth. Makow had never had a drink like this before.

MacGinity watched Makow and smiled. "Ya like it?"

Makow nodded.

Lame Beaver gulped his down in a few swallows. "Good cider, MacGinity. So, did you pull the other tooth the next day or did your son?"

"Mark? No, that boy wouldn't help me out like that. I don't think he would help me out if I were drowning in the lake. I pulled me own tooth the next day, and soon everything was right as rain. Just got me a big hole now."

Makow listened and wondered why this man's own son would not help him.

"MacGinity," said Grandfather with a smile in his voice, "more cider?"

MacGinity poured more of the sweet liquid into Lame Beaver's cup. Then he tipped the jug to his own lips and gulped some himself.

"My friend, why do you think your son would not help you?" Lame Beaver asked curiously.

"Well, ya see, Mark is me boy, but he isn't me son. We are not of the same blood, him and me.

"You see, I came upon him when he was a wee babe. His da was a trader with the Hudson Bay Company, a Scotsman like meself. I never knew his ma. In fact, if I didn't know better, I would say he never had one unless it was a she-bear.

"His da was lost to smallpox and lay weak and alone in his cabin because no one would help him. Everyone was afraid of that cursed and deadly disease."

"I do not blame them," said Lame Beaver. "I lost my woman to the pox. It is bad medicine."

"Aye, 'tis true, but from inside the cabin I could hear the squalling of that boy. He had the lungs of a wild animal calling for help. I couldn't take it no more. When I went into the cabin, I found him in a cradleboard, hanging on a peg. He smelled bad, as he had been thar for two days. His da had passed by that time.

"I took the boy from the cabin and lit a torch to the old shack to burn out the disease. From then on the boy was mine."

Cradleboard? thought Makow. Could it be that his enemy had Indian blood, blood like his own?

"The boy was on a cradleboard?" asked Lame Beaver.

"That he was. Wrapped in moss and rabbit fur and tied in a leather cover. I had to cut away the cover as it was so wet and soiled, and the child was covered in boils."

"Had he the disease?" questioned Lame Beaver.

"No, boils from his own stink that burned his skin. It took a long time for him to heal. I tried to put him in a proper home with a woman to care for him, but everyone knew he was the son of the Scottish trader that died of smallpox. No one wanted him."

"It is a surprise you and the boy did not become ill," said Lame Beaver.

"I had the blasted disease soon after I arrived in Montreal. But it did not affect me so bad. I guess I am just too mean for the disease. They say once ya had it, ya can't catch it again.

"I think because the boy was up on the peg and not handled, and tightly wrapped in the cradleboard with only his face peering out, perhaps that saved him. Perhaps he smelt so bad those pox couldn't tolerate him. He was watched out for, that one."

"Was the trader's woman Indian?"

"I do not know, me friend, but do not say that to the boy. I never have spoken to him about this as he sees himself as my son. The subject of the cradleboard has never been mentioned."

"Where was this trader's cabin the boy came from?" asked Lame Beaver.

Makow glanced up and knew what Grandfather was thinking.

"His father was one of the first traders with the

Miami, along the Beautiful River. He fought with the English against the French, for a while, I was told. I suppose it was Ohio."

Lame Beaver looked across the top of his cider mug to Makow, who breathed a slow sigh of relief knowing his brother had been taken at Detroit.

"The Beautiful River sounds like a nice place to be from," said Makow.

"The Beautiful River was well named by the French as it is beautiful," MacGinity explained. "I heard it said the French once thought that river was the prized Northwest Passage, until they discovered it fed into the Mississippi. That's where I understood Mark's da was headed, to trade along the Mississippi. Poor devil, he didn't make it."

Makow finished the last of his cider. He had heard enough of the story of his enemy. He wished he could tell the boy about his cradleboard, but for the sake of MacGinity's friendship he would not.

"Makow, ya should go walk around the fort and take in the sights if ya like. Thar is no danger here, just watch out for yar friends, the Sauk. Ya might even run into Mark."

Makow looked at Grandfather to make sure it was alright with him, but planned to avoid ever seeing that boy Mark again.

Grandfather smiled. "Do not be gone long as we still have a long paddle."

Makow nodded and left the men to their stories.

*Chapter Nineteen*

# ANGELIQUE

Outside the cabin, Makow decided to continue following the road that had led them to MacGinity's cabin. He made his way past French and Canadian traders chatting together and voyageurs lying in the shade of the trees, until he came to the end of the road and another gate that led outside the palisade. A small building towered high above the gate, with several soldiers standing guard inside, watching out over the forest and fields.

Outside the walls of the fort was an open space bordered by pens of chickens, cows, pigs and oxen. A large field of corn stretched beyond the pens to the forest line. Makow could see two English women, wearing their long, heavy skirts with aprons, and several small children working with the animals.

Makow turned and reentered the gate. The sun beat down into the fort, where the high walls kept the cool breezes from blowing in. The open gate provided the only opportunity for the wind to stir the air within.

The heat and sweet cider made Makow thirsty, so he made his way through the fort looking for a well, for a cool drink of water. Soon finding one, he lowered the wooden bucket on its rope and cranked it down into the deep hole. When the rope straightened and pulled tight with the weight of the water, he turned the crank again and brought up the cool water from deep below. Lifting the bucket to his mouth, he drank the cool water, splashing some onto his face and down his bare chest.

Just then, Makow felt a hand on his arm. Startled, he pulled back, dousing himself with water. As he wiped his face with his arm and ran his hand over his wet hair, he discovered a very pretty young girl standing beside him, smiling

"Use this," she said, holding out a long-handled dipper. "They do not like that we drink from the bucket. The English think we give each other illness if we drink from the bucket."

Makow took the dipper and smiled at the girl. "Miig-wech," he said softly as he felt his ears and cheeks grow red with the gaze of the girl.

"Ma-how," she responded.

Makow looked at her again. She knew his language, but she was dressed like a French girl with a long skirt and apron, and a short vest. Her eyes were as dark as two blackberries, he thought, and the two braids that hung on each side of her shoulders, with ribbons holding them, were as black and shiny as a crow's wing. Makow gulped as he realized this was the prettiest girl he had ever seen.

The girl giggled and reached her hand up to Makow's hair. "Did someone try to take your hair?" she asked as she gave it a gentle tug.

Makow looked around and hoped no one had seen her do that.

"*Je m'appele* (my name is) Angelique."

Makow was now puzzled. He had heard similar French words from the traders around Detroit. Was the girl French or Indian? he wondered.

"Oh, pardon. My name is Angelique," she said, thinking that Makow might better understand English. "I live with the de Langlade family. I am their servant."

Makow looked at her intently, unable to think of anything to say.

"And your name, monsieur?"

"Ah... Ah... Makow... they call me Makow," he stammered, looking down at the girl's feet.

The girl again giggled. "For a moment I thought you had no name. It is my pleasure to make your acquaintance. You are Ojibwa from the Minissing

Michilimackinac, oui?"

Makow shook his head, "No, Odawa."

"Oh, from L'Arbre Croche?"

Makow scrunched up his face. "No, from Detroit. My grandfather and I are on our way to Wa-gaw-naw-ke-zee."

"Oh, so you are on your way to L'Arbre Croche, I see."

"What is that Lobe Crounch?"

"It is Crooked Tree, French name, you know, for your Wa-gaw-naw-ke-zee."

"Oh," said Makow nodding his head. "Your de Langlade, this family you live with, is French? You French?" he asked.

Angelique lowered her eyes and softened her voice. "De Langlade, he is a great trader and fighter for the French. His mama is Odawa like you. His papa was French, from Trois-Rivières, like his wife. He fought the English, a long time ago. He led your people against them in a place along the Beautiful River.

"And I am...," she hesitated as she looked up and past Makow. Then she quickly turned away and lowered the bucket into the well.

"Angelique? What are ya doing talking to this Odawa?"

Makow turned and saw MacGinity's boy, Mark,

standing behind him.

"Me-cow, I see ya made it to the fort. What do ya want, to beg more food from me father?"

Pretending not to hear, Angelique continued to crank the bucket down into the cool, deep well.

"Angelique, did ya hear what happened yesterday?" asked Mark.

"Non, monsieur, I did not," she replied as she pulled up the full bucket.

"This Odawa here was surrounded by Sauk when me father and I saved his life. If it wasn't for me, he wouldn't be here this day. Ain't that so Me-cow? Mooo-cow? Mooo," said Mark laughing loudly.

Makow cleared his throat and quietly agreed, "Yes, you are right in what you say."

"I saved his life. What do ya think of that, Angelique?" questioned Mark.

Angelique shrugged and pulled the heavy bucket of water to the edge of the well. Makow reached over to help her, touching her hand in the process.

Mark watched the two closely, and his muscles tightened with jealousy and anger. For two seasons he had tried to make conversation with this girl, something the Odawa had managed to do in minutes.

Angelique wiped her hands on her apron and turned to Mark. "What do I think, monsieur? I think you brag too much," she said sweetly with a smile and pulled the bucket towards the jug she was trying to fill.

Makow snickered while helping Angelique with the bucket.

"Oh, I see how it is. Yar kind stick together. I bet you thought this pretty girl was a Frenchie like yar old man, didn't ya Me-cow? Well, she ain't. She's a Pawnee, captured when she was still in a cradleboard and stolen away by the Sauk from beyond the Mississippi. Me father told me she was bought by de Langlade in Detroit as a servant. So she's not even as French as you. She's just an Indian servant."

Angelique tried not to listen and fought back her tears.

"And this metis here," Mark jabbed a sharp finger into Makow's shoulder, "he's on his way ta L'Arbre Croche for his time of seeking."

Mark laughed loudly in Makow's face. "Seeking! Seeking! Looks ta me like yar seeking a Pawnee." With that comment, Mark shoved the bucket of water out of Angelique's hand, throwing her water jug to the ground and chipping it.

Makow turned in anger and jumped at Mark, the two tumbling to the ground. Soon they were a knot of arms and legs, struggling in the dirt and creating a cloud of dust.

Angelique reached out to stop them, but was pulled away by the arm of de Langlade.

"Let 'em fight. It's good for 'em." He laughed heartily, sticking his clay pipe into his jagged teeth.

Angelique picked up the chipped water jug and ran back to de Langlade's cabin.

Soon a crowd of soldiers, Indians and traders gathered, laughing and hollering at the wrestling boys. A Sauk, excited by the action, gave a war-whoop that brought more of his brothers.

MacGinity heard the sounds of rushing moccasins along the gravel road in front of his cabin and wondered what was the cause of the commotion.

Sticking his head out the door, he saw the gathering crowd. "Looks to be some wild cats goin' at it, Lame Beaver. Let's have ourselves a see."

Caught up in the fun of his new friend, Lame Beaver sprang to his feet and followed MacGinity out onto the crowded road. As they approached, there was so much dust in the air, MacGinity was sure two great Scottish traders were wallowing there. Lame Beaver circled around the well just in time to see his grandson pull Mark to his feet, only to yank him around and tumble to the ground again.

"Hey, Scotchman, you need to teach dat little boy

of yours some of de tricks you know," called the voice of de Langlade over the shouts and cheers of the crowd. De Langlade gave a hearty laugh and blew smoke from his pipe into the air.

Pushing through the crowd of cheering voyageurs and Indians, MacGinity pulled the two boys to their feet and separated them. Both struggled to free themselves and finish the battle. Lame Beaver, too, pushed his way to his grandson, shocked and ashamed of his actions.

"He started it! He started it!" screamed Mark with blood, sweat, and dirt covering his face. "I saw him trying to bother Angelique. Ya saw it, didn't ya de Langlade?"

MacGinity turned to de Langlade.

De Langlade threw one of his hands up in the air and pulled the clay pipe from his teeth with the other. "Scotchman, that is not what I see with deez eyes. I see your boy push de bucket from my servant Angelique's hands. I see de Odawa try to help her. Oui, it is true, dat Odawa he make de first move, but to help Angelique."

Lame Beaver took Makow by the arm. The boy's wild hair was full of dirt, and blood ran from his nose.

"Be off with ya!" shouted MacGinity to the crowd. "We'll handle this." With that command the crowd of men began to disperse.

"That Pawnee is to blame!" shouted Mark.

De Langlade walked over to MacGinity and Mark. "Dat Pawnee is named Angelique and is a member of my household," he snarled down at Mark. "Remember dat, MacGinity's son! You English think you can get away with everything."

"That's enough, de Langlade, I'll be takin' care of this," growled MacGinity.

"Dat is good, Scotchman. Do so before the Indians decide to take care of all you English." De Langlade blew a defiant puff of smoke from his pipe in the direction of MacGinity.

"MacGinity, I am sorry for the anger between my grandson and your son. I think Makow and I will leave now to Wa-gaw-naw-ke-zee before more trouble happens between these two. You will go west to Rainy Lake soon. I probably will not see you again in this lifetime."

MacGinity released his hold on Mark, and the boy dusted the dirt and dry grass from his clothes and wiped the blood from his lip onto his shirt sleeve. "Now go to the lake and get cleaned off," MacGinity ordered the boy. "Then we'll be doing some talking."

As Mark stomped off MacGinity turned to Lame Beaver. "It is a sad way to say goodbye. I am ashamed of me boy."

"Yes, I am also ashamed," Lame Beaver agreed as he nudged Makow. Makow looked up at the bear of a man who had befriended them, but no words would come. Finally he offered his dirty arm to MacGinity.

MacGinity took Makow's arm and shook it. "Makow, always remember, peace is better. It is a lesson you boys both must learn."

How could MacGinity be so good and Mark so bad? wondered Makow.

"MacGinity, good luck in the west. May your canoe touch no drifting logs or sharp-toothed rocks, and I hope you visit me someday."

"I would do so, Lame Beaver," smiled MacGinity, "but I think the boy and me will never paddle this way again."

MacGinity took Lame Beaver's arm and shook it, then slowly turned and walked toward his cabin.

## Chapter Twenty

# WA-GAW-NAW-KE-ZEE

Makow held his head tall as he walked through the fort. He knew he should not have fought with MacGinity's boy, but how could he be at peace when the boy wanted war? Makow now would take the punishment of his grandfather's shame with him as they left.

Outside the fort, Mark crouched down over the water with his shirt off and washed his swollen wounds in the cold lake. Grandfather and Makow passed by without a word, and Mark did not look up.

Beyond the corner of the fort, Makow could see their canoe turned upside down with their belongings packed under it.

"Go wash," instructed Lame Beaver.

Makow kicked off his dusty moccasins and waded out to his waist along the rocky shore before plunging head first into the water. He swam a few strokes and then stood and washed the dried blood from his nose. He dunked his head over and over, trying to wash away the dust and blood and anger.

When he finished he walked ashore, shaking the water from his head in every direction.

"Oh! S'il vous plait! Please!" announced a voice. It was Angelique.

Makow stopped at the edge of the water and quickly tried to smooth his hair.

Angelique's blue skirt and apron were splattered with water. They both laughed. "I am so glad you have not left yet. But it is good you leave. I have heard de Langlade and the others at the cabin say that there is much trouble on the wind. Trouble for all."

Makow had not heard Bwondiac's name mentioned since they arrived, but perhaps now, he thought, a belt had found its way to the Ojibwa.

"Now you will go to L'Arbre Croche for your time of seeking. That is good. I am only sorry girls do not have to seek. I brought you something to thank you. Mark is such a bother to me. I just want him to go away."

Angelique held out her hand and presented Makow with a rock. "I know of rocks and the sweat lodge. This is from me."

Makow looked down at the round rock. It wasn't as big or heavy as the other rocks, but it had just become his most important one.

"Miig-wech, Angelique."

"Bon voyage, mon ami (Good journey, my friend)." She smiled and turned back toward the fort.

Makow stood and watched as Angelique walked down the beach. Lame Beaver jabbed him with his elbow and smiled. In his hand was a dusty crow's feather that had been lost in the scuffle.

Makow, still astonished by Angelique's generosity, took the feather from his grandfather's hand.

"Look, Grandfather," he said. "She brought me a rock for the sweat lodge."

Grandfather laughed and rubbed his hand in Makow's hair. "Nice gift. Pretty girl. She reminds me of your grandmother." He chuckled and walked to the canoe, carefully turning it over and checking their belongings.

Makow carefully placed Angelique's gift with the other rocks, and then stuck the crow's feather behind his ear .

Lame Beaver directed their canoe out onto the water where he held it in the waves while Makow loaded it, placing his rocks, one by one, into the center of the canoe, making sure Angelique's small rock was on the top of the pile.

As the two took up their paddles and pushed out along the shore, Makow turned and looked back at the fort. There stood Angelique at the gate. She gave Makow a small wave of her hand and disappeared within the fort.

Makow smiled. He had never felt like this before. Actually, he could not remember looking at a girl before, although he had talked and played with many as he grew up around Detroit. But to really look, this was new.

As they began to paddle west, Makow and Lame Beaver passed a neat row of small cabins at the edge of the settlement. Something there caught Makow's eye. Suddenly he recognized Mark, running from between the cabins out into the water, holding the bottom of his shirt up, as if carrying something in it.

Lame Beaver saw him at the same time and directed the canoe away from shore into deeper water. When Mark was nearly hip deep in the water, he pulled a rock from his shirt and hurled it toward their canoe as hard as he could. Then came another and another.

"Here are some more rocks for ya! I saw Angelique give ya one, now go sweat!" Mark yelled.

Angered, Lame Beaver dug deep with his paddle, pulling the canoe farther away from shore as the rocks plunked in the water all around them. Makow paddled harder, and the two moved onward away from

Michilimackinac and Makow's enemy.

"I do not know what has made MacGinity's boy so angry in his heart. He does not know himself, only his anger," insisted Lame Beaver.

Makow nodded his head. "He doesn't seem to get along with anyone, not even MacGinity, who is good to him."

"You see, this is what happens when there is trouble and confusion in a land. Families are broken apart. People lose themselves. This is why your mother and MacGinity say peace is better. And this is why your mother insists on finding your brother."

Makow turned his thoughts to his mother. Suddenly he was lonely for her words and instructions. She was always trying to teach him about life and people, even people like the English, whom he did not know or understand. After having met MacGinity, he could see the worth of this man. But now, Makow wondered, what would his mother say about Mark? How should he treat such a boy? Was it because Mark had no mother to guide and raise him that he acted this way?

Soon the two paddled on towards Wa-gaw-naw-ke-zee. The sun was low in the western sky, making the surface of the lake sparkle and gleam like many watery stars. The forest passed before their eyes along the shoreline. Trees crowded trunk to trunk connected the blue sky with the blue of the water, ba-esk-ko-be, Indian blue. Here and there, rolling slopes of sand drifted to meet the water's edge. In the distance to their right, Grandfather pointed out a long line of green islands and called out their names: Woman's Island, Medicine Island, Beaver Island.

Makow strained his eyes against the sun's reflection to see them. It seemed strange to him that the sinking sun was now on their right. The water seemed slightly different here, too, perhaps lighter to the paddle. And below, in the cool clear water, he saw a fish nearly as big as a man swim under them. A gentle bump from underneath made Makow wonder if a giant fish such as this could overturn them.

Makow began to grow anxious. They were nearing their destination, and Grandfather began to paddle faster.

"Grandfather," asked Makow, "tell me of this place. Why is it called Wa-gaw-naw-ke-zee, Bent Tree?"

Grandfather thought back to his boyhood. He breathed the cool, clean air of his past and smiled as he told the story.

"When I was a boy, the Odawa lived at Minissing Mackinac and around the place of the fort. For many years we grew only corn on our land. Then the land grew tired, and the corn grew no more. Men and women were sent in many directions to find a new place for us to grow our corn. Soon we found this place and moved here when I was a young man."

"But Grandfather, mother said you had your time of seeking at Waug-o-shance when you were my age."

"That is true, but our people had not yet moved our village along this shore. It was shortly after I met your grandmother that our people built here. But our people knew of this place even before the smallpox raged upon our land.

"The French from the fort often joined us here to help us clear land and plant. The traders came and so did the Jesuits, leaving their old mission across the straits at Saint Ignace. The village grew and stretched for many miles, all the way from A-na-me-waa-ti'-gwenh (Cross Village) to We-que-ton-sing (Harbor Springs)."

"But why the name Wa-gaw-naw-ke-zee, Bent Tree?" questioned Makow.

"When our people first found this place it called to them from the water. On a very high bluff of land stood a great tall pine. Its body was perfect, but the top of its branches were crooked and bent, bent by the hands of **Nan-o-bo-zho** who had bent the tree to mark a place for his people. The tree was near the center of Wa-gaw-naw-ke-zee at what is now Cross Village or Middle Village."

Makow watched the shoreline and finally Wa-gaw-naw-ke-zee began to reveal itself. Ribbons of smoke curled from tops of lodges all along the shore for as far as his eyes could see. Still, he could not see a bent tree on a high bluff.

"Does the tree still stand?" asked Makow as he strained his eyes in his search.

"No, the great tree is gone. The land where it once stood is covered with poison ivy so the people will stay away from this place and let the ground heal."

"What happened to the tree?" asked Makow.

"No one has that answer. Some say Men-o-bo-zo blew the tree down in a windstorm to hide it from the many traders who came to visit. This I do not believe as the traders, especially the French, were always our friends. They bought corn and maple sugar to feed their fur brigades.

"Some say two brothers, in a fit of anger, cut the tree down when their sister left with a French soldier to live at the fort, long ago.

"Others say a warrior, tired in his travels, carried his canoe above his head up the sandy bluff to make a camp for the night. The great branches of the bent tree reached down and grabbed hold of the warrior's canoe and pulled him over backwards, throwing him down the bluff and crushing his canoe to splinters. The warrior was so angry, he took his axe and cut the tree to its very roots."

Makow listened. "So no one really knows what happened to the Bent Tree?"

"Yes, that is right."

The bluff of white sand soon appeared before them, but Grandfather continued directing them on to Waug-o-shance.

"Grandfather, do we not make our camp at Wa-gaw-naw-ke-zee?" asked Makow, hoping to see the old village where his grandfather once lived.

"We will see the village after your time of seeking. Now it is time for you to find your place, the place that you and the earth feel most comfortable together."

Makow shivered as he realized his vision-quest was about to begin. The two continued to paddle until a point of land stuck out from the shore. The sandy beach covered with trees and grass looked welcoming to Makow.

"Makow," called Lame Beaver, "we are here."

Fighting the waves of early evening, they brought the canoe as close to shore as they could and unloaded their belongings. Makow helped pile their things together on the shore, being especially careful not to misplace the rock given to him by Angelique. Then they carried the canoe from the water and high up onto the stone-littered sand.

Makow watched Grandfather limp across the beach and knew he was tired.

## Chapter Twenty-one

# WAUG-O-SHANCE

Once ashore, Makow opened the sleep mats and blankets in the shelter of a high bluff. His grandfather followed the wooded trail that led up from the shore and collected dried pine and pieces of bark to start a fire. When the old man returned, Makow pulled his box of flint and steel from his travel pouch and cleared a place for the fire.

Seeing what Makow was about to do, Lame Beaver shook his head. Laying down the wood for the fire, he found his neatly packed bundle of board, block, and bow, now dried from its wash in the lake.

"This is an important time for you, Makow. I would like to make sure we do things as our elders would have done, long ago.

Makow nodded and together he and his grandfather worked the bow and fed the tiny wisps of blue smoke until a small fire grew.

They pulled out the last of MacGinity's dried venison and bread and made their meal.

"Tomorrow we search the woods for what will be

needed. I must find the herbs to make your fasting drink, and you must find what you will need to make your camp."

"Grandfather, when do I begin to find my place?" Makow asked as he watched Grandfather carefully bite down on a piece of dried venison. Makow was tired from the journey and the incident at the fort, and he hoped he would not have to hike deep into the woods this evening.

"Tomorrow we will rise early and search the woods for food. There is no need for a great amount of food, for in the evening you will begin your fast. I will stay here in camp, and come to you once a day. We will not speak, but I will bring to you water and a brew made of herbs that will help you keep your strength."

"Grandfather, who did these things for you?"

"It was done differently then. When I was near your age, my grandfather brought me here, and then he returned to Wa-gaw-naw-ke-zee. He arrived back here to this very shore three suns later and took me back to our camp where I had my sweat."

Makow thought about the old ways and was glad to hear that Lame Beaver would stay near. Perhaps as a young warrior his grandfather felt more comfortable alone at this place because it was the land of his people, Makow decided. He knew he did not wish to be so alone.

"Grandfather, at the fort, the girl, Angelique..."

"Ah, the Pawnee girl," interrupted Grandfather. "It was a thoughtful thing to bring you a stone for your sweat lodge. Though it is small, I am sure it will glow bright in the fire."

"Angelique said girls do not have a time of seeking. Is that true?" questioned Makow.

"Have you ever heard of a girl seeking?" responded Grandfather.

"I never wondered about it before. Why do they not seek?"

"There are many reasons. One reason is that girls will have their own special time. Among our people, girls go to Woman's Island with their sisters and grandmothers. There the women teach them the many things they will need to know about being a woman.

"But the most important reason girls do not have to seek is because they are not like men. They are a people apart from men and do not have that need. Women are special creatures. They were made with many gifts that even the bravest warrior will never understand."

Makow listened closely.

"Many snows ago my grandfather told me that

men, like all the great two-legged and four-legged creatures, even like the winged ones and the green ones, are Beings.

"Women are not Beings. They are Creators. They have the ability to make life, to nurture life, and to do many things all at the same time. It is a gift.

"Have you not noticed how your mother can care for our lodge, weave, tan skins, prepare our food, take care of our sicknesses, and still be able to sew moccasins for Gladwin, and all the time, seek after your brother?"

Makow agreed, although he didn't understand.

His grandfather continued, "Makow, at the time your mother is doing all these things, what is it that you do? What is it I do? I walk with the old men of the camp, perhaps I fish. When I was younger I would hunt and trap."

Makow interrupted, "You were also a warrior and a runner."

"Yes, this is true. But I was seldom called upon to do those things. A man's life, often, is not as busy as a woman's. There are many things she can do, all at the same time. Women are a different people. It will take you many snows, like it does all warriors, to understand these things."

"So because of this, she does not have to seek?"

"Because of this, things seek her. She will always have a path to follow."

Makow never thought about his mother like this before, but now that he did, he decided it was true.

Makow's thoughts returned to his own seeking. He wondered what it would be like searching for his place in the woods. How would he know the right place? What would be the sign? It was much like seeking his brother. How would he know? What would be the sign?

"Grandfather? Will you tell me how I will know where to make my camp for seeking?"

"This is a simple thing. You will look for your place in this world."

Makow was puzzled by this answer. He reached up to his crow's feather and gave it a tug, making sure it was still there.

"Have you ever walked or paddled your canoe and seen a place so full of beauty that it felt like you belonged there? It is a place like that you will seek, a place where you feel close to the great Mother Earth. That will be your place."

Makow smiled. He had felt like that before and knew it was a special gift of beauty. And it had surprised him that he had a similar feeling when he met Angelique. Now he wondered if he would feel something like that if he met his brother.

"Makow, now I need to tell you of your brother so that in your time of seeking, you might have better understanding."

Makow sat up straight on his mat. Had his grandfather read his mind? He tucked his legs tightly under him and listened. His grandfather reached over and fed the small fire several pieces of dry wood. As he waited for the fire to grow, he pulled his warm English blanket close around his shoulders.

"Makow, from the time of your birth and that of your brother, you were both very different. You had a loud voice most all the time. Your brother was quiet and only loud when he demanded something. When you were born your skin was light. Your brother's was darker. Your eyes, the color of fawn, your brother's the color of charcoal. Your hair, though dark, was still lighter than your brother's and curled upon your head. Your brother's was like a raven's wing and lay flat. It was strange to all, how two who held hands before birth could be so different."

Makow listened carefully. So in his veins the French blood did run first. It was strange to him that he had been raised within his mother's lodge while his brother, taken by the English, looked more like an Odawa.

"There was something else, Makow, that made your brother different from you," continued his grandfather. "When he was first born your mother noticed this, and it filled her with great fear. She knew that there would be great trouble between her sons in the future. It was only after your brother was taken that we began to hope that this difference would be a good thing that would protect him and lead him back to his people."

Makow was silent.

Lame Beaver sat up straight and pulled his blanket away from his shoulder. The campfire light shone on his sagging skin. "Makow, what is it you see here upon my skin?"

Makow looked at his grandfather. "It is a tattoo placed there by my mother."

"Yes, that is true. What is the design of the tattoo, Makow?"

"It is the design of two bear claws. A sign of power and protection."

"That too is true, Makow. But it was also the scar that was upon your brother's shoulder at the time of his birth, a design I had your mother place on my shoulder in the very place as your brother's. It was a sign of remembrance, so when he came back to us we would know him."

Makow stood on his knees and leaned over to look closely at his grandfather's tattoo. It was as if two perfect marks of the powerful Makwa, the bear, were placed there.

"This, Grandson, is why you were named Makowaian, Bear-skin, and your brother Nin Ki-kin-awadji." Grandfather looked deeply into Makow's eyes as he watched him repeat the name.

"Nin Ki-kin-awadji. *I Am Marked?*" Goosebumps ran up and down Makow's spine as he repeated the name. Nin Ki-kin-awadji, the name of his brother.

Makow looked silently at Grandfather, not knowing what to think. Makow had seen this design from the time of his early childhood. It was placed upon his knife sheath, it was beaded into the designs of the moccasins his mother made, and it was also upon Grandfather's shoulder. Why had he never been told its meaning? Makow felt anger and resentment build within him, for not being trusted with this story.

"My brother must have great power and strength to have such a design upon his body," said Makow. "More power than his own brother who does not even look like his people." Makow stared into the flames of the burning fire, feeling suddenly alone.

"Makow, why would you say such a thing?" questioned Grandfather.

Makow did not look up. His heart filled with jealousy. "My brother, he is important. He carries the power of the bear upon his shoulder. That is a powerful sign."

"Yes, Makow, but how do you think your brother received this sign? This scar?"

Makow scrunched up his face. He did not understand.

"Makow, it was you who was with him from the time of his beginning. That is why you have the name of the bear: Makwa."

Makow slowly looked up at Grandfather. What did he mean? Why did he call the sign a scar?

"It was you," said Grandfather slowly, "who fought with your brother, even before your birth. This is why you were not told of all this until now. This is why your mother was so full of fear to have you know of your brother and why she worked for the English, to seek information to give to you. Now it is your time to seek peace, even though your brother was your enemy before your birth."

Makow quickly rose to his feet in anger. "How can this be? Why was I not told? You have kept my own story from me, and now you tell me my brother was my enemy before our birth?" Makow could feel the hurt burn his eyes.

"Makow, I too am tired and worn by the trail of this life. Do not be angry with your mother or me!" begged Lame Beaver, feeling the boy's spirit cry with hurt.

"Your way of thinking, yours and my mother's, is old! It is like the bow you make your fire with. This is not my way, Grandfather. I do not believe your way of thinking."

"Makow, it is time to rest. You have much to dream on..."

"Dream? Dream? How can I find sleep now, after you have told me that I carry so much anger toward my brother that I scarred him before we were even born. As if I tried to take his life before he walked upon Mother Earth. How could this be?"

Lame Beaver reached out his arm to his grandson to try to sooth his pain.

"Just leave me alone! I do not want to hear any more of your stories, Grandfather."

Makow could not control his feelings and fled from Grandfather's fire into the darkness of the forest.

## Chapter Twenty-two

# WARRIORS

Makow ran from the camp, following a trail that led into the dark, deep forest. His eyes burned with tears and his heart was heavy with hurt and resentment. He knew he should mark a tree or break a branch to help him find his way back, but at the same time, he felt that he never wanted to return. How could his own family have thought such things of him—that he carried with him an anger so deep that it was there even before he was greeted into this world?

Makow knew the design—the scar—upon his brother's shoulder was not put there by him. That was the old way of thinking. He knew his brother would never be found, nor would Makow seek this one who was so special, more special than himself. One that was even more Indian.

Branches and bushes tore at Makow's skin and yanked at his hair. The crow's feather, knotted firmly, stayed close to him as he ran still deeper into the woods. It wasn't until the great net of the spider caught him in its grasp that Makow stopped running.

Fighting the sticky pull of the net that covered his body, Makow plucked and pulled strands from his face, mouth, and arms.

Finally, in frustration, hot tears broke and he sobbed in the silence of the purple shadows. Makow knew he had lost his way...like he had lost his family. All that he had once known to be true was now something different. The voice of the crow no longer called to him, and all around he felt the eyes of night creatures staring at him in his sorrow.

Wiping his eyes and nose, and pulling the last of the spider's web from his face, Makow turned in circles, lost, wondering where he was. Staring up through the dark shadows of the tree branches, Makow looked to where the sky was the lightest. That would be the direction of the great lake. But he did not want to return to Grandfather's fire. He must now find his own place and make a new story. His own story.

Soon Makow could hear the buzzing of mosquitoes, and in a moment a nation of the evil flying warriors tried to land and sample his blood.

Makow worked frantically to protect himself from the attack, swatting and slapping. He began to run again through the dark woods, escaping his enemy. As he ran he tried to shield his face from the bushes and branches that poked, gouged, and dug at his skin. Finally, exhausted, he came to a stop and stood silent in the woods. He was even more lost and confused than he was before.

Makow leaned against a tree and took deep breaths while he waited for his heart to stop beating so loudly in his ears. As he began to calm himself, he thought he could hear something.

Holding his breath so he would not make a sound, Makow heard branches breaking in the distance and the pounding of moccasins on the forest floor. Filled with fear of what might be lurking just beyond in the darkness, he listened intently. Soon, he heard the voices of young men, and war cries echoing in the forest, making his blood race with fear.

Looking upward to find the lightest sky, he began running toward the lake. He soon reached a high sandy bluff where the wind blew softly and the waves washed upon the shore below. This was not Grandfather's camp, thought Makow, as he looked around for the tiny light of Lame Beaver's fire.

Makow stood silently, straining over the sounds of the waves to hear the warriors that haunted the forest. But there was no sound of them at all. Had he imagined them? Was it just his own fear that filled him with so much fright?

Makow waited and listened for a long time, but there were no more war cries, not even the hooting of an owl. Makow dropped to his knees in the soft, cool sand and decided this was the place he would rest for the night.

His mind filled with emotion and sorrow, he worried about his grandfather being alone by his fire. Makow knew the old warrior was probably worried over him. Still Makow knew he could not go back, at least for this night.

Without flint and steel or sleep mat, Makow had to find a way to make himself warm and comfortable. He dug a circle in the sand and removed rocks. From a nearby cedar, which did not have the prickly needles of the pine, he pulled fragrant branches and laid them in his nest, to protect him from the sand's dampness. Then Makow remembered the teachings of his grandfather. He did not want to give up the protection of his crow's feather as an offering this night, so he pulled strands of hair from his head and placed them at the base of the tree.

Makow then crawled into his nest and used some of the branches to cover himself. Crawling under the boughs, he sought the dreams that would help him understand all that had happened that day.

Makow wondered if the shouts of the warriors

were real. What would they have been doing in the woods? It hardly seemed possible. Soon the soothing sounds of the lake were joined by the calls of the screech owl as it stood guard over Makow in his loneliness.

The next morning, before the sun painted the sky with light, Makow awoke to the soft sounds of moccasins in the sand. Lying silently in his cedar nest, it took him only a moment to realize they were drawing near. Jumping to his feet, he threw back his branches. There, standing in the dim light of morning, were four young warriors, hovering over him like shadows.

He knew they were not much older than him, but they were painted and dressed for war. Makow turned within their circle. It was as if he had been captured by the Sauk, again.

"Who is this stranger?" asked one of the boys to the others. "What right has he to sleep upon this land?"

Makow was shocked. He understood them! They must be Odawa, he thought, and he breathed easier.

"I am Makowaian—Odawa," he said, trying not to show fear.

The four boys looked at each other, startled.

"If you are Odawa, where are you from?" one

asked.

"You are not from our village of Wa-gaw-naw-ke-zee, or we would know you."

"I am Odawa from Detroit."

"Detroit!" cried one in a voice of excitement.

"Bwondiac!" cried another and gave a war-whoop that echoed into the woods.

"Yes, Bwondiac," agreed Makow. "I heard him there not many suns ago."

"You heard the great war chief Bwondiac? Tell us his words," they insisted.

"Is he a great warrior as tall as the sky?" asked another.

"Bwondiac is a great warrior, but no taller than the average man," answered Makow.

"You lie! He is as tall as the sky. I have heard stories!" insisted one of the boys now so close to Makow that he could smell the dried venison on his breath.

One of the young warriors reached out and touched the crow's feather still knotted in Makow's hair. "The sign of a storyteller. Perhaps you are telling us a story now."

The young men all agreed and laughed.

"It is not Bwondiac's body that makes him tall," continued Makow , "but his courage. It is his courage that is as tall as the sky, or taller."

The warriors stood silent for a moment and then cried their war-whoops into the morning light and danced about in excited agreement.

"Why is it that you are here if you heard Bwondiac before he went against the English at Detroit? Why did you not stay there to run the English out of our land?" asked the warrior closest to him.

"Are you a friend of the English? Do you flee like a rabbit from the sun?" questioned one who had remained quiet until then.

"My Grandfather, Lame Beaver, has brought me here, at this time, for my seeking."

The young warriors all grew quiet in respect. "So is it here that you found your place, upon the sand?"

"No. I walked in the woods too late into the darkness and lost my way. I have yet to find my place. My Grandfather stayed upon the beach near a bluff to make our camp. I should find him now."

The young warriors looked at one another in surprise.

"How can it be, Makow, that you come from Detroit and do not know the plan of our people? How can it be that this was the time chosen for your seeking? Your people must think you are a child that must be kept safe."

Makow felt the emotions and anger of the previous days rise in his blood again. Standing tall, he tightened his muscles, showing he was willing to fight if he had to, to prove his courage.

"Odawa, brother, is it not in your blood to want what is yours? Is it not in your blood to want to drive the English from our land, or do you have friends that are English?"

Makow thought for a moment about his grandfather's friend MacGinity and his enemy, Mark. "No, I have no friends among the English!" he replied firmly.

"That is good! Today, at Fort Michilimackinac, a plan has been made by Bwondiac to help celebrate the English king's day of birth. After today, it will forever be remembered and celebrated by our people." The eyes of the young warrior glistened in excitement, and his friends called out war-whoops in anticipation.

"There are but a few English soldiers that live at the fort, and they will be easily overcome at this celebration. Come join us in our canoe. We go to the fort this day to help give the old English king his gift."

Makow listened and his thoughts drifted to Angelique and the de Langlade family.

"Is it only the English you seek? What of the others who live at the fort?" questioned Makow.

"It is only the English we seek—now. If the others make way for us, there will be no harm that comes to them. Join us!"

Makow breathed a sign of relief for Angelique. Now he understood what she had meant when she said there would soon be trouble.

"At the fort," continued another warrior. "We will trick the English with a game. Our brothers the Sauk and Ojibwa are already there. It is only the Odawa that do not gather. Our O-ge-muk (leader) feels the insult of the Sauk and Ojibwa for not being asked to participate in the game. He has another plan for after the battle."

"But we will not wait," insisted one of the young warriors. "We will play this game, too."

"Will you join us against the English? Against your enemy? Or will you stay here with your grandfather, seeking, like a child even during a time of trial for our people?"

Makow's heart pounded and he was silent for a moment. He thought of Grandfather, probably still asleep in his warm English blanket upon the bluff. What would Grandfather say? Makow knew he would say the same thing his mother would: *Peace is better.*

"We must go! The game will start before the sun is standing still at the top of the sky. If you have but one enemy who is English, you owe it to your people."

Makow thought and thought. The words of his grandfather and his mother seemed old and meaningless. He must now hear his own words. Makow watched as the young warriors ran down the sandy bluff to a canoe they had hidden under a pile of brush along the shore.

"Have you no English enemy?" called one of them to Makow.

Makow hesitated as the face of Mark appeared before him. "Yes!" shouted Makow. "I will go if I may have the one I seek."

Quickly Makow ran down the bluff and joined the boys as they lifted their canoe onto the water and fought the waves with all their might, making their way to Fort Michilimackinac.

Along the waterway in the dim morning light, they soon passed the high bluff that Makow recognized as the place where he and Grandfather had made their camp. It was the place where he had learned his story and that of his brother. Not wanting to reveal his grandfather's location, Makow looked away as he paddled in time with the other warriors. Silently, he worried for his grandfather's safety.

Makow received a sudden sharp blow to his ribs from one of the paddlers, urging him to keep up the pace. Quickly Makow dipped his paddle and again fought the water, leaving Grandfather behind, alone, asleep on the sand.

They had not gone far when a canoe appeared along the horizon. It was heading toward them from the direction of the fort. None of the young warriors broke their pace, and the distant canoe pulled away, to avoid contact.

As they passed in the dim light, Makow could just make out the shape of two paddlers, and on the bow, the sign of the peace pipe.

MacGinity! thought Makow, and his enemy, Mark. What were they doing so far from the fort? Had they heard of the plan? Were they running away? Makow smiled to himself. This was a better victory for him, having his enemy run from danger like a coward.

Just then, Makow felt another sharp pain in his ribs from the paddle of the warrior behind him, pushing him into the sunrise.

Makow secretly was glad the Scotsman, MacGinity, had escaped, but it was bitter to lose the one he was seeking.

### Chapter Twenty-three

# FAMILY

Long after Makow had run into the woods, his eyes full of tears and anger, Lame Beaver sat around his fire and wondered if he had done what was right, telling Makow of his story. But he also knew it was time for the boy to know. And now it was time for him to be alone. The forest would take care of him, here in this place of his ancestors, and perhaps there were even more lessons here for Makow to learn.

Lame Beaver thought it was the ko-ko-ko of the owl that called him from his sleep early that morning, but when he heard the voice of his friend MacGinity, he thought it must be a dream. But above the sounds of the waves washing the shore below, Lame Beaver again heard the great Scottish voice of MacGinity call out to him.

Lame Beaver pulled himself to his feet in the cool blue morning sand. The old man, worn by the night's sadness, peered into the dim morning light and saw the shape of two people bringing a canoe ashore.

"Lame Beaver! Are ya up thar?"

A feeling of dread passed over Lame Beaver as he thought about MacGinity and his boy. Surely, MacGinity knew that Mark would not be welcome in his camp. There must be a very important reason for him to come this distance.

Lame Beaver wrapped his red wool blanket around his shoulders. Standing near the top of the bluff, he called down to his friend, "MacGinity, I am here!"

The shadowy forms paused for a moment. Then one dropped the bow of the canoe upon the sand and began to run toward Lame Beaver. The old man, concerned about this action, returned to his fire and placed more wood there, waiting while his visitors came to meet him. When he looked up from the light of his campfire, he saw the face of his daughter.

Frozen in his movements, Lame Beaver wondered if this was the trick of an old man's eyes. But no. Standing beside her was MacGinity.

Lame Beaver and Wild Rose embraced. Tears of happiness ran down the old man's cheeks. He had not dared to hope that he would ever see his daughter again in this world.

"So, Lame Beaver, again you owe me for a gift!" announced MacGinity .

"MacGinity, I owe you much."

The trader extended his hand to shake Lame

Beaver's arm, but Lame Beaver pulled MacGinity close with a hug. "My friend. My friend."

Wild Rose smiled and reached for her father's hand. "Has Makow already left for his place in the woods?" she questioned.

Lame Beaver looked sadly into the fire as they all sat on the mats to talk. He told them the story of the night before, but expressed hope that Makow would soon make his way back to his campfire.

MacGinity looked puzzled but remained silent as Wild Rose began to tell her story. She said she had left their lodge that day in Detroit and made her way through the crowd to the fort. There she found Major Gladwin and delivered both his moccasins and the warning, but Gladwin gave her no news of her son.

"That night," Wild Rose continued, "word was sent out among the people that Gladwin would not allow more than six warriors at a time to enter the fort. It seemed the wise Major Gladwin had heard the singing of the bad bird and called his men to arms, closing the gates and watching the people closely.

"Bwondiac knew someone must have told of his plan and soon learned of my friendship with Gladwin. He was about to pay me a visit when I pulled my canoe upon the water and left Detroit. Some nights I found the places where you and Makow had camped, and even the broken berry bushes from which you ate.

"Alone I could not paddle quickly enough against the wind and knew I would never catch up with you until I made it to Waug-o-shance. When I arrived at the fort last night and sat around the fires of the Sauk and Ojibwa, I heard the story of a young Odawa fighting the English all by himself. I thought nothing more of it until one mentioned the boy was lucky to have kept his teeth after the scuffle, unlike the old man he traveled with. It was then I knew it was you they were talking about."

Lame Beaver ran his tongue over the broken edges of his teeth and into the gaps in his gums and began to laugh. "So you found us because of my teeth?"

"I was told Makow fought with the red-haired trader's boy."

"Aye, and that is how she found me. Me hair," added MacGinity with a wink.

"Where is your boy?" asked Lame Beaver, although glad Mark was not there.

"He chose to stay at the fort and promised not to get into any trouble. There is supposed to be some type of goings on at mid-day. A game of baggataway. I promised him I would be back in time, but that wasn't good enough for him. He wanted to stay.

"We passed a canoe full of young braves going back toward the fort not long ago. I suppose they were Odawa wanting to play in the games against the Sauk, too."

"Where did you pass these braves?" asked Lame Beaver.

"Just up the shore, not more than a half pipe away. You know," said MacGinity, "it was hard to tell in the dim light, but I thought I spied Makow in that canoe. With his bushy hair all cut jagged like it was, I thought for sure it was him."

Wild Rose turned to MacGinity. "What do you mean, hair cut jagged? Why did you say nothing to me?" she questioned MacGinity.

"Because it be dark, because I wasn't sure," he answered. "Because you were excited to see your father and son."

Lame Beaver could see the fear in his daughter's eyes. She stood and looked into the woods, then turned to Lame Beaver and MacGinity.

"Makow was not so upset that he would have left, was he?" she questioned Lame Beaver.

"It would not be like him, you know that," he answered. "But I did think he should have returned to our camp by now. Daughter, do not be alarmed."

"You do not understand. At Detroit it has been said

that the English forts will fall with the first move of Bwondiac, on the birthday of the English king. If Makow has returned to the fort, he will be caught up in this rebellion."

MacGinity jumped to his feet. "Mark!"

"You say they plan a game of baggataway this day?" asked Wild Rose.

"Aye, it is in celebration of King George's birthday. That is why Mark wanted to stay at the fort, so he wouldn't miss any of it."

"We must go!" Wild Rose rushed to the canoe as Lame Beaver put out the flames of the fire.

MacGinity pulled the canoe from Wild Rose as she struggled with it. Lifting it high upon his shoulders, he made his way to the water. Wild Rose and Lame Beaver carried the paddles. All three knew it would take hours to get to the fort, but they also knew they must try. The sun was now rising and the wind blew with them and gave them speed. There was no time to stop, but they took turns resting, keeping the canoe in constant motion.

Tired and thirsty, they finally approached the point of land near the French cabins, where Mark had bid them goodbye with his rocks the day before. It was then they heard the blast of a cannon and the "Huzzah!" of the soldiers.

"It is for the king," called MacGinity as he plunged into the water to pull the canoe ashore. Grandfather stepped out and Wild Rose helped MacGinity pull the canoe onto the sand alongside another canoe, one that had just been carried ashore by five young Odawa warriors.

Once on shore, they followed the isolated trail that cut a path through the forest. The shadows of the forest soon gave way to bright sunlight and rows of tiny green corn plants. It was then they heard the first cracks of the flintlock rifles from the fort.

"That's not the sound of baggataway," cried MacGinity. Afraid for the life of his son, the trader rushed toward the fort.

Wild Rose ran out ahead of her father, through the rows of young corn. There in the cornfield something caught her eye. Wild Rose stood for a moment and watched. Suddenly, a black crow flew out of the forest directly over her head, cawing loudly. Lame Beaver caught up with her just as she bolted after the crow.

Lame Beaver called to MacGinity and motioned for him to follow Wild Rose, who ran in the opposite direction.

As he fled the fort holding Mark by the hair in one hand and a rock weapon in the other, Makow saw same crow. But all his attention was directed on yanking Mark through the cornfield away from the danger of the battle at the fort. The boy, not understanding that Makow was trying to save his life, turned on Makow, shoving him to the ground and grabbing the rock.

MacGinity, seeing his son, ran past Wild Rose and hollered, "Mark! Stop!"

"This will be the last fight I'll have with ya!" shrieked Mark as he turned on Makow.

"Mark!" yelled MacGinity, "I'm here!"

Mark paused for a moment when he saw MacGinity running toward him with Wild Rose and Lame Beaver.

"They broke into the fort, Da!" he shouted. "The Sauk and Ojibwa, they broke into the fort and—" Mark could not describe what he had seen. His emotions were out of control, and he turned and flew at Makow with the rock held tightly in his hand.

Lame Beaver, overcome by rage, pushed MacGinity aside and rushed toward his grandson. Pulling Mark off Makow, the old warrior threw Mark to the ground and lunged toward him.

"Father, no!" shrieked Wild Rose as she ran into the circle of anger.

Makow's heart leapt at the sight of his mother,

and he knew then what he had to do. In an instant he yanked away what was left of Mark's shirt to reveal the scar of the twin bear claws on his dirty shoulder.

Suddenly everything stopped.

Wild Rose gasped in shock, understanding now what Makow already knew.

Lame Beaver froze, his eyes wide with recognition. This boy, this enemy, was the grandson he had sought for so long?

MacGinity looked into the faces of the others, confused by their reactions.

Finally, Wild Rose spoke with tears in her eyes. "MacGinity, this boy, your son, his true name is Nin Ki-kin-awadji. Your son, he is my son, too."

"Nin Ki-kin-awadji," she said softly, turning her attention to Mark. "Do you not know your own mother?"

Horrified, Mark hid behind MacGinity.

Renewed war cries and rifle blasts from the fort demanded their attention. The air over the fort was thick with gray smoke.

"We must go," said Wild Rose. "I have lost my son once, I do not wish to lose him again because of war."

Wild Rose turned to Makow, throwing her arms around his neck and holding him tightly. "You have found that which you were to seek," she whispered.

"I knew it would be you who would find him."

"This is all too much to understand," interrupted MacGinity. "But we need to go now, if we are to escape at all."

The five of them ran from the cornfield to the sandy path, following it back to their canoes. Makow saw the canoe belonging to the young Odawa warriors and hoped only for peace for them all.

The five climbed into MacGinity's canoe with the sign of the peace pipe. Makow slid over, allowing his brother to kneel beside him, and handed him a paddle. Makow could see Mark's anger had faded to confusion as tears rolled down his cheeks. My brother, thought Makow, knowing he would now have to make a place of peace for him in his heart and in his family.

As they pushed off, leaving the anger of battle behind, they paddled together towards the safety of Waug-o-shance, a place of seeking. Along the shoreline, Makow spied a crow, the storyteller, perched upon a great rock. Reaching to his dusty, chopped hair he touched his battered and dirty crow's feather still knotted there. The crow fluttered its wings as they passed and cawed to the family that had just found itself,thanking them for another new story to tell. "A-ho!"

# Glossary

**A-ho**. An exclamation meaning "Let it be" or "It is so."

**Baye of the Punts**. The area known today as Green Bay, Wisconsin.

**bozhoo**. A greeting.

**Bwondiac**. The proper pronunciation of the Odawa chief commonly referred to as Pontiac. He encouraged the Indian Nations to join together to fight the British in 1763 in what became known as Pontiac's War or the Beaver War.

**capote**. A coat made from a wool trade blanket and often worn by fur traders.

**Fort Michilimackinac**. A fort located at the northernmost point of the Lower Peninsula of Michigan.

**gunwales**. Top rim along the edge of a boat or sailing vessel.

**kinnikinnick**. Also called Indian tobacco. A mixture of bark, dried leaves, and sometimes tobacco.

**La Grande Rivera**. Known today as the Grand River.

**Lake of the Illinois**. Known today as Lake Michigan.

**metis**. A person who is part French and part Native American.

**Minissing Mackinac**. Known today as Mackinac Island.

**mocock**. An Indian container or basket woven from natural materials or shaped from bark.

**Nan-o-bo-zho**. A hero character who did both good and foolish things. Various names and spellings are found in Indian stories for this character.

**Neolin**. Delaware prophet (religious leader) that tried to stir up confusion and promote rebellion against European settlers.

**Odawa**. Proper spelling for the Algonquian Indian tribe known as Ottawa.

**On-on-ti-on**. Iroquois nickname for the French governor, meaning Great Mountain.

**O-wash-ten-ong**. Known today as the Grand River.

**pemmican**. Dried meat, fruit, nuts, and berries mixed with bear fat.

**queue**. A braid of hair worn hanging down one's back.

**River Ouisconsin**. Known today as the Wisconsin River.

**Sau-ge-nong**. Know today as Saginaw.

**smallpox**. Contagious disease that spread through North America upon the arrival of Europeans. Approximately one-third of all people that caught smallpox during the 1600s-1800s died.

**travois**. A bed or carrying apparatus made from long branches that form a frame and that is pulled by hand or behind a horse.

**Wa-gaw-naw-ke-zee**. Algonquian for the location of Bent Tree.

**wampum**. Beads made of shell which were strung or sewn on to things. Used ceremonially and also as a medium of exchange.

**wattape**. A twine-like string made from the roots of a tree.

**Waug-o-shance**. Algonquian for Place of the Fox.